IN THESE TIMES THE HOME IS A TIRED PLACE

STORIES

IN THESE TIMES THE HOME IS A TIRED PLACE

STORIES

JESSICA HOLLANDER

2013 WINNER, KATHERINE ANNE PORTER PRIZE IN SHORT FICTION

University of North Texas Press
Denton, Texas

10 9 8 7 6 5 4 3 2 1

Permissions:
University of North Texas Press
1155 Union Circle #311336
Denton, TX 76203-5017

The paper used in this book meets the minimum requirements of the American National Standard for Permanence of Paper for Printed Library Materials, z39.48.1984. Binding materials have been chosen for durability.

Library of Congress Cataloging-in-Publication Data

Hollander, Jessica, 1982– author.
[Short stories. Selections]
 In these times the home is a tired place : stories / by Jessica Hollander.—First edition.
    pages cm—(Number 12 in the Katherine Anne Porter Prize in Short Fiction)
Katherine Anne Porter Prize in Short Fiction, 2013
  ISBN 978-1-57441-523-0 (pbk. : alk. paper)—ISBN 978-1-57441-538-4 (ebook)
 1. Young women—Fiction. I. Title. II. Series: Katherine Anne Porter Prize in Short Fiction series ; no. 12.
  PS3608.O484554A6 2013
  813'.6—dc23
                                    2013028386

In These Times the Home Is a Tired Place is Number 12 in the Katherine Anne Porter Prize in Short Fiction Series.

The electronic edition of this book was made possible by the support of the Vick Family Foundation.

Cover and text design by Rose Design

To Richard,
an expert at combatting exhaustion

Contents

Acknowledgments

Deep gratitude and acknowledgment is given to the following publications, in which these stories originally appeared, sometimes in slightly different form: "You Are a Good Girl I Love You" in *West Branch*; "If We Miss the Beginning" in *Pank*; "This Kind of Happiness" (as "Not a Family") in *Phoebe: A Journal of Literature and Art*; "I Would Stop" in *Sonora Review*; "What Became of What She Had Made" in *The Journal*; "The Year We Are Twenty-Three" in *Hayden's Ferry Review*; "March On" in *Quarterly West*; "The Good Luck Doll" in *Corium*; "In These Times the Home Is a Tired Place" in *Web Conjunctions*; "How To Be a Prisoner" in *The Emprise Review*; "Like Falling Down and Laughing" in *The Cincinnati Review*; "I Now Pronounce You" in *The Normal School*; "Buttons" in *Alice Blue Review*; "January on the Ground" in *Sou'wester*; "Ruckus, Exhaustion" in *New World Writing*; "Staring Contests" in *Frigg*; and "The Problem with Moving" in *Big Lucks*.

I would also like to thank everyone who supported me and my development as a writer. First, thanks to Katherine Dunn and those at the Katherine Anne Porter Prize and the University of North Texas Press who generously brought this book into being.

Thanks so much to all the editors who included these stories in their magazines and showed continued enthusiasm for my writing, including Michael Griffith, Matthew Pitt, Roxanne Gay, and Mark Cugini, and to Richard Thomas, for thinking of me and including my work in his anthology of provocative women.

To my parents Tom and Cindy Hollander, who instilled a healthy skepticism, and to my brother Daniel, who rebelled and became a romantic.

Special thanks to Wendy Rawlings for invaluable meetings and discussions about these stories, and to Michael Martone, Kellie Wells, Kate Bernheimer, and all the writers at the University of Alabama's MFA program who pushed me outside my comfort zone and taught me that writing can be many things, and one of the things it can be is fun.

To others who have helped me improve these stories, particularly at Sewanee Writers Conference and Rope Walk Writers Conference, including Christine Schutt, Padgett Powell, and Benjamin Percy.

To other mentors who have helped me on this path, particularly at the Sewanee Writers Conference, Rope Walk Writers Retreat, and the University of Michigan, including Christine Schutt, Padgett Powell, Benjamin Percy, Kevin Wilson, and Laura Kasischke.

To my friends who have grown with me and inspired me for years and years, especially Liz Diamond, Katy Hunsche, Lara Hillard, Ben Goldman, and Mara Gaviglio.

To Lynn and Harold Maurer for their support and savvy.

To Shannon May for the artwork covering this book.

And finally, thanks to Richard for his endless support, and to Oliver for every day pulling me back into the world outside my head.

You Are a Good Girl I Love You

A note posted on my fourteen-year-old sister's door, a warning: *Our house has walls and doors like any other house and inside each house are rooms and inside the rooms are beds with covers and no matter how much you kick the sheets mom shrink-wrapped to the mattress the covers are heavy on a chest.*

My sister's explanation for why she now slept on her bare mattress naked.

p.s. if this is a problem i will gladly sleep clothesless in the backyard.

My father pounding on the door yelling Beatrice If I'm Late and Beatrice You Think I'm Impressed You Are A Child. He dropped us at school since my sister ditched from the bus stop every day for a week, so I took my time getting ready: putting on makeup and blotting it off. My father wanted order and my sister systematically disordered. It was a home theater Mom and I gossiped about in the driveway and stairwell: who had said, who had shifted, who had asked us to communicate something.

Dad found me finished in the bathroom and said, "Please deal with your sister."

It wasn't really a show. A sister naked first thing in the morning became daily—her flat on her back, sprawled human-sacrifice style; her frightening ribs, her raised stomach—it wasn't healthy. Most mornings she sat up slumped, head down and moaning, and I pulled a T-shirt over her head.

1

Today her deadheaded boyfriend in boxers—Thank God—
and knee-high gray socks. He lay passed out on the floor with a
three-foot extravagantly dirty bong inches from his fist. The window open and the smell of coal made the room cold and stuffy; it
was snowing. My sister already dressed on the bed laughed at my
face. "Let's make Dad later than late," she said.

"You've gotten lazy," I said. "Every morning the same franticity
and all the cars are bitches."

Beneath us the front door slammed and the boyfriend's foot
twitched. We waited and heard the door open again and my Dad:
"Gertrude! Drag her down by the greased strings she calls hair!"

Bea held my hand; I sat beside her on the bed. "I think it
helps his productivity at the office," she said.

I hoped the result would be a car for my eighteenth birthday—
for taxiing purposes.

—◊◊◊—

I was dragged into it. I was allowed to do what I wanted; Bea
wasn't allowed out until her dirt-creased boyfriend showed
some respect, like Please Sir and Thank You Very Much This
Is Delicious—it had come to this. "I want my house a Victorian sanctuary," Dad said, overheard in the entryway when I was
just back from work. Beside me Bea's boyfriend against the wall
with his hands in his pockets and his eyelids lowered sleepily.
He resembled somewhat a dream-teen actor, the one skinny and
long-haired and shuffling. Bea's boyfriend was eager to drop out
of school and move to California, where he could pose for pictures
on Hollywood Boulevard with Superdog and Mr. Impossible and
The Hulks.

Mom watched me from the piano bench like Move Slowly,
and soundlessly I slipped off my boots.

"I want everyone who enters mannered and buttoned-up,"
Dad said.

Bea shouted, "You don't make Gertrude's boyfriend present cows or wear frock coats or bow in doorways."

"Gert's boyfriend doesn't come in the house with cigarettes. He doesn't make comments about her legs licking his lips."

"Repression screws people up psychologically," Bea said.

I jumped, feeling the boyfriend's hands on my shoulders. He helped me out of my coat. He hung it on top of other coats; the whole wall was puffed with suede and down and faux fur. "Thank your dude for me."

I'd seen this idiot at my boyfriend Pete's locker; they shook hands and Pete gave me a look like This Is Crazy I'll Tell You Later. But Pete was SAT-determined and afternoons his parents concealed his phone and closed the wood shutters of the bedroom window I usually snuck in. We didn't mind sneaking around. Mostly we studied together or whispered about the future or had sex quiet beneath the covers.

Neither Pete nor I had much contact with Bea's boyfriend besides a nod or smile-sneer. We generally figured he'd wind up in the sewers, a good-looking troll that would make others believe life beneath the bridge preferable.

The boyfriend smoothed my knee-length coat to the bottom. "In health, Bea's researching the female orgasm," he told my mother. "Expect a call about it."

"Beautiful," she said.

"I've got to depart," the boyfriend said. "My dad's just like him."

"We're talking about a free humanity," Bea told Dad in the kitchen. "Why must we wear coats when it's cold and buy food in packages?"

"That's the language of vagrants," Dad said.

"Because I'd like the option of wearing a halter top in December."

I sat beside Mom on the piano bench. "It's gotten to the point," she said. "Some lightening up may be necessary."

"Because the street's always looking for more homeless and think how attractive your legs will look wearing a trashcan," Dad said.

There was a commotion, furniture moved. Then Dad leading toward the stairs with Bea's arm tight in his grip and Bea crying furious, lock-jawed.

"Close the door to your room and knock yourself out," Dad said. "Scream, strip, smear Crisco in your hair. Knock yourself out."

—᠁—

Coaxing Bea from her room wasn't difficult: she was starving and eager to stare blankly at objects and ignore everything Dad said. Mom appreciating our new Victorian sanctuary came to dinner in her puffed-hourglass dress she never thought she'd have an excuse to wear again, with pearl buttons up to her chin. Dad made a show unfolding his napkin. It wasn't a good conversation. Dad calling Bea's boyfriend a Hyde and Mom mentioning her waist felt caught inside a paperclip.

"The parlor was full of visitors today," Mom said. "They brought news most intriguing."

"No more about Bea's boyfriend," Dad said. "He's banned from discussion. I want to hear about this trip."

Next week Pete and I were taking his family's Jeep to visit campuses. Of course Pete and I would attend the same school, live in the same dorm, plan classes to start and end together so we would be only briefly apart. We had a dependable timeline mapped out behind the child's armoire in his room involving dates: graduations, wedding, first jobs, first house, babies raised by smiling parents. Some evenings we practiced smiling thinking the more one does it the more natural it feels.

"Who's chaperoning the trip?" Dad asked. This after weeks saying only I Hope You Don't Dumb Down Your Chances For That Guy.

"I'm pretty sure your time warp is limited to this house," I said. "Queen Victoria died in 1901."

"I think there should be a chaperone."

Bea opened her mouth and a wad of chewed chicken and potatoes plopped onto her plate. She was really a child. Looking at her—tallness and slicked hair—I kept forgetting.

"I just mean we can try for some mannered living," Dad said.

"It's a very tight space for women," Mom said. "But the parlor is lovely."

Bea dropped another chunk of food on her plate.

"This is a joke." Dad put down his fork.

"So laugh," I said.

"I wouldn't appreciate an anarchist *son* either," he told me.

Mom patted her hair, stood, and swayed. "One thing about Victorian women is they knew how to exit. Big grand exits." She waltzed toward the stairs. No one laughed.

I took Bea's plate to the sink and covered the chewed chunks with a napkin. Bea picked at her teeth.

"That's great," Dad said. "Dinner's over. The worst time of day with nothing to look forward to."

—⋙—

Bea helped me with the dishes. The day faded, and Dad made coffee and sat on the back porch in full winter wear watching the neighborhood kids run off their last bits of energy: throwing mittens and stomping hats and dashing in and out of imagined boundaries. The coffee steamed and Dad huddled over it.

Mom reappeared loosened in sweatpants with a pencil in her hair. She paused next to me and looked out the window.

"Great entrance," I said.

"Well, I'm a human again, not just a woman." She sat cross-legged at the table with her crossword.

"I can't even watch television with him," Bea said. She had her phone out, distracting her from loading the dishwasher. "People kiss and he's all 'Is that really necessary?'"

"He liked you better when you were little," Mom said, looking through the glass door at Dad like we didn't all prefer littleness to big and awkward.

"We liked him better then, too," Bea said.

"No one wants more adults in a house," Mom said.

Bea threw her phone against the wall.

Mom picked it up and set it on the table. "Beatrice, show some restraint."

Bea slid open the glass door and stood one leg in the kitchen and one on the porch. "I'm going to have a baby." She looked at the back of my father's head. "Pete and Gertrude are going to raise it."

—⬩⬩⬩—

I tried—grabbing her arms asking What Baby Beatrice You Are A Child—but she fought me off leaving me looking at my parents and them looking at me like What Are We Going To Do This Girl Is Crazy.

Bea locked herself in her room with a dresser against the door; we listened to it sputter dragged above us.

Dad left the kitchen, and Mom followed him repeating Wait Stop What. In front of me there was a door, and through backyards I could run coatless and shoeless to Pete's where stacks of flashcards lined his desk waiting for me to quiz him, and beneath his bed lay a basket of thick warm socks.

Dad returned with an extra scarf wrapped around him and said Gertrude You Are A Smart Girl I Love You. He walked out the backdoor toward the thin patch of woods and the backyard of another house similar to ours—with more walls and doors and beds, etc.

"It's a joke," I told Mom.

"Or she thought the truth would be funnier." She shivered. Cold air blew in at us from the door Dad left open. "I should be more a mother. There was so much fathering I figured it wasn't necessary."

I closed the glass door and looked for Dad in the dark yard. He wasn't there. "This house needs someone stationary."

"Maybe you missed your sister's announcement." She got a sponge from the sink and walked around with the rough end scrubbing phantom spots on the counter. Then the table. Besides seeing photos of her young and Bea-like, I didn't usually notice how old she was. Her hair grayed and now she looked more like me.

"I didn't miss it," I said. "I'm deemed fit to mother."

Mom scrubbed a yellowed place on the floor. "Dad would like to come along next week." She shifted, crouched and determined above the spot. "He wonders about Pete's influence over your decisions."

"I don't need you guys worrying about me."

"You think we can worry nonstop about your sister? We'd never get any sleep."

—ᗺᗺ—

Calm, I just wanted to keep moving. Upstairs, my door locked and the house quiet, I couldn't wait not knowing if Dad was home. Through the window I climbed down the lattice and saw Bea's boyfriend shuffling across the street. I met him at the bottom near the ropey dead vines. For how locked-up Dad wanted the house, his night surveillance was lazy. It was snowing again so no footprints to worry about, and no cold ground crunch.

Bea's boyfriend stared at the snow when I said Give Me Your Cigarettes And Drinks And Anything Else You Know

What I Mean. What worried me: he handed over his cigarettes and lighter.

I jogged to Pete's house on the snow-fluffed sidewalk. Our neighborhoods overlapped each other, all quiet streets and thick old trees hiding various denials of boredom. Everyone Victorian and mannered and buttoned-up except wine bottles overflowed recycle bins and condom rappers stuck to sticks and beneath the snow there was evidence of dogs allowed to go on the sidewalk.

Passing the park of nautical-themed playground equipment, I saw a figure on the largest boat. Ten feet off the ground, he climbed over the navigation wheel and up the wood slats. My bundled father. He jumped ship. He hit ground and lay crumpled. Probably he didn't notice me in my black sweatshirt. I kept jogging, watching until he sat up and waved, and I waved, and then he was behind me.

Pete's house was a ranch and his room in the back. He sat blanket-wrapped in the window. He was tall and too-angular with big features always a little red and a little happy even when he was sad. He lowered himself into the snow when he saw me.

"If you want to say abortion go ahead," he said. He helped me through the window, and we fell tangled onto his bed; it was covered in cut index cards—pink, green, yellow—with my hand-writing scribbled *Gainsay. Amalgamate. To leave suddenly.* They were scattered all over the room as though thrown.

"Abortion," I said. "I'll talk to her." Bea wasn't going to ruin my life to make some kind of statement. I pulled the flashcards closest to me and stacked them.

"I just thought the two of them and the poor kid," Pete said.

"A kid's not something you can hide in a dorm room and sneak out for bathroom breaks."

He sat up serious. "Obviously we'd get an apartment. We'd schedule it out."

"You're joking," I said. But I knew he wasn't. "This isn't our time to raise some baby." I went around his room gathering flashcards, explaining I'd Like To Do Things How They're Supposed To Be Done I Thought That Was The Plan. I went around his room gathering flashcards because that was a priority—because the words felt big and grand stacked neatly in my hand.

If We Miss the Beginning

If it doesn't stop snowing will we miss the beginning? If we miss the beginning and if the beginning is what matters should we encourage the snow and say sorry it was the snow? If the groom gave better directions would we be there already and would the boy stop crying and would we not have to miss the beginning? If the snow stops and we've already missed the beginning can we go to the café we went to as kids? If the café reminds us of our own beginning could it count in a way later when we explain to the groom why we missed the beginning? If inside the café the snow starts again and we see the snow through the window and understand the beginning is the only thing would it change the end? If we stay in the café in our beginning could we say to the boy there will be no end? If the snow doesn't stop and we never make it to the wedding and never say to the groom congratulations on your beginning we wish it was ours would no one see with the ending so close how impossible the beginning is for us to see?

This Kind of Happiness

In the middle of a mandatory meeting about proposal distribution, the girlfriend excused herself, took the stairs to the second floor bathroom, where space belonged to her: all these cubes she could enter, doors she could latch. Here, she could carefully read the directions and administer the test. She could sit on the toilet watching the white stick's cloudy window without the boyfriend asking, asking, asking. What's that? What's wrong? Are you . . . ? Are you?

At home, the boyfriend was everywhere. He occupied the bathroom with her—flossed while she showered, shaved while she peed—because, he once told her, the windowless, linoleum-floored room, with the ceiling fan cranking and the curling water streaks and the clumps of hair in the corners, was the loneliest room in the apartment.

The girlfriend went into a bathroom stall and took the pregnancy test. She waited. The bathroom door opened and a pair of red Mary Janes paused in front of her stall.

"Do you mind if I get on the phone?" the shoes asked.

"I guess not," said the girlfriend.

The shoes walked away, and then shortly: "I meant to wake you. I want you to be a thick-tongued idiot when I tell you if I'm driving and I see you in the street, I'll smash you into a fire hydrant."

The girl in the red shoes laughed.

Two pink lines made their way to the stick's surface. The girl-friend stuffed the test into the trash receptacle.

When the girlfriend exited the stall, the red-shoed girl stood stooped with her elbows in one of the sinks, looking in the mirror. "He's a puddle I keep slipping into," she told the girlfriend.

The girlfriend nodded. There were a lot of puddles. Big ones were easy to avoid, but small ones seemed a moderate challenge. People walked right into them.

—ɯ—

Already, the girlfriend's senses seemed heightened to damage. She avoided coffee in the morning, tuna at lunch. Hot tubs could injure the embryo; strenuous exercise and soft cheese, too: she recalled these things she'd read or heard or imagined. She moved slowly around the cold apartment, crossed the icy drive with her puffy-mittened hands in front of her like she wanted the world to pause. Wait. Hold it. She inched forward.

On their food-stained loveseat, the girlfriend sat down with the boyfriend. He pressed his lips together. She knew he had his suspicions. They'd been reckless with protection: a test-tube experiment. Maybe, maybe, maybe. They were, after all, in their late twenties with no reason to move further down the path of Standard Expectations. But the path was there: in the increased telephoned pleadings from parents, in the pictures of wedding-cake smiles and babies-in-beanies their co-workers posted in the office. The girlfriend and boyfriend hovered before the paved path shaded by thick-trunked trees, lined with trim grass and manicured mansions, where miniature houses played mailboxes and animals played lawn ornaments and people played happiness.

She told the boyfriend, "Don't be angry or nervous or excited." She suspected all such reactions were momentary and dishonest, learned responses to what had happened to millions before. "There will soon be a reason," she said, "to go down the toy aisle at the supermarket."

The boyfriend nodded. "That is not an inconvenient aisle."

They shifted so slightly their ankles touched.

The boyfriend asked, "Will you marry me? Should we buy a house?"

The girlfriend shook her head. She did not like being referred to as "the girlfriend." She knew the boyfriend found this amusing, but was also hurt by it, and it was for both reasons he called her the girlfriend all the time. Meet my girlfriend. My girlfriend likes boiled chicken. My girlfriend's feet are always cold. He forgot her real name.

But fiancée would be worse; wife: the worst. They had crossed over the threshold and could run down the path if they wanted. The girlfriend felt like hobbling around the entrance for a while.

—ɯɯ—

The boyfriend watched family sitcoms with a notepad before him, sniggering and jotting things down like *father: clumsy (trips over tricycle—should look at the ground), mother: stupid (bright-eyed— need clothesline, oven mitt).*

The laugh tracks bothered the girlfriend. Sometimes she came into the living room just so she could boo when the laughter started. She was sick of everything. She threw up all the time.

The boyfriend frowned at her. "You're ruining it."

"That's not a family," the girlfriend said. She pointed at the black and white figures. She stood in front of the television and smiled broadly, lifted her eyebrows, then pretended to lay fish forks at a table. The girlfriend wore an apron and high heels. The girlfriend applied makeup for only her husband and children to see. She was beautiful.

"I watch modern ones, too," the boyfriend said. "I want a comprehensive sample."

The girlfriend stood stiffly in front of the television. "Maybe we can raise the kid like this, in thirty-minute segments, where we stop his accidental involvement in a cock-fighting ring with a friendly parent-to-parent chat. We buy him a new hat in the last four minutes, and the kid smiles. We send him off 'til tomorrow."

"I've nowhere else to look," he said. Growing up, the boyfriend's ripped-clothed, long-haired parents had slept in different rooms with different people. They all lived in a crumbling house filled with kids kicking cans, flipping furniture, and cheering anarchy in their underwear in the street. Now his parents were recovered. They all lived alone and slept with each other and only tentatively left home to work or visit their grown children, who they encouraged gently to show them how wonderful family life could be.

On the screen, a mother smiled over a tennis shoe, her delicate hands crafting a double knot with floppy loops. "Now be home before dark," the screen said.

"There's got to be a middle ground," the girlfriend said, "between this kind of happiness and your kind of suffering."

"You don't realize there's a lot of scenarios." The boyfriend looked at the screen and wrote something down.

The girlfriend left the room. "Just mute the volume," she called. "I don't need to hear how hilarious my life's about to be."

—◊◊—

Her parents said: "Take vitamins every day and don't stuff yourself like a pig. The more cereal you eat the more likely you'll have a boy." They clipped pertinent articles about baby hangnails and diaper bags bursting, sent them to the girlfriend in an envelope with money stuffed in: a crumpled hundred, a few fifties. They called her together, the father upstairs on the green rotary, the mother cordless in the basement, her feet propped on collected *Better Lives and Gardens*.

"I'll still be a dad," the father said. "But I like the addition of *grand* to the title."

"Will the baby sleep in a closet?" the mother asked. "Or the kitchen?"

The apartment the girlfriend and boyfriend shared was very small. The carpet flapped in corners; they strung sheets over doorways in place of doors. There were cracks in the ceiling through which centipedes and furry spiders crept.

"This is where we live," the girlfriend said.

Her parents said: "It's time you became owners instead of renters."

"Does the boyfriend have a fear of commitment?" the mother asked.

"I told you he was a street-jumper," the father said.

"He's educated," the mother said.

"You can be more than one thing," the father said.

Her parents said: "That boy's the father. You can't unmake him that."

—w—

While the boyfriend watched sitcoms in the evening, the girlfriend sat on their small slab porch, entertaining the image of a frazzled single mother: pushing a stroller down an icy street with plastic grocery bags hung from the handles, the mother's frame obscured by a fat purple coat, huge boots, and shoulder-slung duffels. This seemed a heroic image. "Single mother," she whispered to the frosty wind, and although muffled by the scarf wrapped tight across her cheeks and mouth, she liked the way it sounded.

Through the thin wall, she heard the boyfriend laugh. He had discovered closed-captioning; he no longer took notes. He recounted whole shows to her, and when she told him to stop, he developed this pleased, distant look, and she knew he just recounted the episodes in his head.

"They feel like my friends," he told the girlfriend later, in bed. He yawned happily and placed his head in her lap, and she stroked his long black hair and didn't let a single strand fall forward to tickle his face while he slept.

—⚍—

The baby grew. The girlfriend wore big jackets to the office and hunched over hoping no one would bump into her. She was quiet at work, a non-nuisance. Professionally dressed, hair-bunned, high-heeled: a respectable administrator of other people's problems. "Just tell me what to do and I'll put it on your desk."

She wanted to have the child, wanted to raise the child to be exactly like her, like all those fervent religious people got to do, except she would use logic instead of faith. Don't you see, child? Doesn't that make sense? Isn't this the way it should be? She wanted to hold that happiness inside, huddle around it like a big fiery secret shared only by her and the child. But there was all this interference.

The baby grew, and when the girlfriend could no longer hide it, her co-workers smiled knowingly and told her dirt-eating, crib-buying, tears-of-joy stories. She nodded politely. Was she excited? Yes, she was exhausted.

All these appointments to keep, various tests and measurements, fingers pricked by women in clown-patterned scrubs, doctors with chalky fingers and smug smiles. It was convenient to attend with the boyfriend. He talked to the doctor, held the girlfriend's hand, suppressed his smiles when she asked him to. "What do you want?" he asked.

He carried all bags and duffels. They bought a stroller, and on the test-run around the block, the boyfriend pushed it down the icy street with the girlfriend unfettered beside him. She bent over the stroller where the baby would be and made cooing noises. She made up a song about how going over the curb was fun. Bump bump up.

The baby grew, the baby grew. The living room filled with laughter.

—⚭—

Then it was spring. There once was a path called Standard Expectations, and this path was paved and kept clean, and every week a maintenance crew came and groomed the grass and trimmed the big shaded trees making passage as easy as possible. Here is the path, the path said. Don't you want me?

Then it was spring, and the boyfriend wanted to get married. "Based on my studies," he said. "As parents, husbands and wives fare better than girlfriends and boyfriends." He quoted several TV shows. He quoted the girlfriend's parents. He quoted the makers of the path. "Besides," he said. "It's a nice picture."

He flipped the channels and showed her clean individuals in clean living rooms and kitchens and backyards, and they were smiling and laughing and even fighting: but that was a part of it, the boyfriend told her. "You throw manila folders and wind-up clocks at each other, and then you go to the bar or your neighbor's fence or brood awhile on the park swing-set, and you come back misty-eyed with your palms turned up." He showed her. "Isn't that nice?"

—⚭—

The boyfriend's parents called. The girlfriend excused herself to the slab porch where the purple-leafed bushes needed a trim and the boyfriend's Morning Glory crept closer and closer to the door.

The air had turned thick and muggy; mosquitoes hovered and darted around her bare limbs. She heard the boyfriend's aggravated voice through the wall: he blamed his life on his parents. Stories tied to every flaw, every mistake. This is why the boyfriend refused to accompany her to the roller rink. This is why when he searched the closet for the garden spade and discovered one of her barely worn patent-leather shoes, he held it in his lap crying. This is why, when particularly upset, the boyfriend shut his eyes and whispered: "I wish I was never born."

The boyfriend's parents wanted to speak to the girlfriend. The girlfriend took the phone and inquired about their jobs in elementary school restructuring and asked if they still liked the shed they'd bought to replace the fire pit in the backyard. They had become good nervous people who wanted to know if they were doing right in the world. "Every day is hard," they said. "Sometimes we wish for a second chance."

They said: "We would be honored if you took our name in marriage."

—⟋⟍—

In the middle of a mandatory meeting about proposal distribution, the girlfriend went to the second floor bathroom and sat in the same stall in which she'd taken the pregnancy test eight months before. Alone with the stale soap smell, the girlfriend whispered all titles available to her. Single Mother. Pregnant Bride. Gun-toting Madwoman. She worried over connotations, paths lined with pansies and dogs that wagged their tails from a distance and never jumped or barked too loud.

The girl in the red Mary Janes came in and asked if she could get on the phone. The girlfriend said fine. She was accustomed to interference. She was ready to hand her life to whoever wanted to take it. If you get bored, pass it on. Just tell me what to do. She served food at a table. She tied shoes. She smiled.

The girl in the red Mary Janes pronounced her vowels with a strain to them, like they were tightrope-walking a very straight line.

"No," the girl said. "Not until you screw me one more time."

"No," the girl said. "There will never be a last time."

The girl laughed and made plans to meet in the alley behind the office. And the girlfriend wished she was the girl in the red shoes. The girlfriend wanted to lie on the gravelly road and fuck some monster, the baby sandwiched between them, jostled, maybe, yet still alive.

When she came out of the stall, the girl in red Mary Janes watched her in the mirror. She looked at the girlfriend's stomach.

"Is the guy in the picture?" the girl asked.

The girlfriend nodded. He was in the picture. They had become the picture. Two parents put their hands on kids' shoulders. Mail slid into miniature houses and then into large ones. Birds flapped around birdfeeders and ants turned away at the door. Home smelled of laundered clothes and gas from the grill on the porch. The sun was so bright the sky filled with overexposure, wilted the corners to orange, to red, to black.

I Would Stop

My spike-haired aunt: the speech corruptor, the hamperer of plans—my mother warned me. At the airport, waiting for me at baggage claim, she wore a papier-mâché parrot. The bird wobbled against her chest. "You can't lollygag at the airport." She squeezed my arm. "Tell me about—"

"It's best—no." I carried my heavy suitcase. With a broken wheel I had no money to fix, I was at the mercy of my mother, who I'd begged for this ticket, who said, "If you must go, go heavy and hobbled."

"We should have met before," said my aunt. Her chin—it was my father's—small and sloped and committed to the neck. She was much older than she should've been.

"My mother," I said.

Her elbow pinned her purse to her side like it was something slippery. "I'm glad to see you're a child," my aunt said. "I only knew your father as a child. He wasn't himself after that—most aren't."

The walk from airport to parking lot: hurried, frigid. We loaded into her car half-full of flimsy and filmy paper: grocery receipts and lost-pet fliers. I stuffed my coat by my feet when she turned up the heat and got us on the highway and drove the wrong way—I knew by the signs; I knew because my mother said specifically, "Ypsilanti, if that's not a town for crazies," which was west and south from the airport. We drove north, north, north.

"Tell me how he was found," my aunt said.

"My mother."

"She told you, yes? Tell me, how did he look?" A myth about his family—the Zarbours—they smiled when they died. Over hotdogs, the night I choked, my father told me I would die, I would stop. He closed his eyes and smiled.

"Do you like living . . . ?" I motioned to the bland highway dotted with snow—it was like a paper grocery bag, molded. I wanted to say something nice. I wanted my fingers to be of use, to feel her chin for stubble.

"I've been proximate to death my whole life," my aunt said. "I could reach out and hug it."

"I came to hear about him."

"He let me speak at the wedding. I was his only family, and your mother—I'm sorry."

My mother had told me: Death should be a mystery. My mother had shrieked: Why do you want to visit your aunt?

"Tell me," my aunt said. "Did he smile?"

Not really knowing—"It was a grimace."

"Show me," said my aunt. "This can be misread."

She watched my face move—it portrayed something; she sighed. Through the windshield: trees smothered by white, the ground pocked and gray. Birmingham—an exit. Texaco, MacDo, stop sign spray-painted "8." Breadcrumbs to find my way back, back, back to my mother.

A hill covered with rocks, an iron gate: a cemetery. An orange cat licking its paw. Black and white and striped, like moving markers, cats darted between graves.

My hand braced the dash; my aunt out of the car before I knew we'd stopped. Like white smoke, the sky was translucent.

"Your grandparents," she said. Two flat stones—charcoaled, sunk in the snow-spotted dirt—she toed them with brown boots; she bent toward them, the Zarbours. Her papier-mâché parrot: too summer for winter, too large against her chest, it wobbled. My spiked-haired aunt: her pale chin, her smile— gorgeous, contagious—it reminded me of someone else.

What Became of What
She Had Made

Lynette hadn't heard from Christine in six months and three days. There'd been something of an argument, nothing abnormal. Her daughter was unpleasant on the phone, and Lynette questioned her about her life and whether she ever planned to take it seriously. She figured stubbornness had kept her daughter from calling her back; or else the phone buzzed in a purse on a hook in the morgue, and Lynette really was a horrible mother. It would be her fault somehow.

She almost called in a Missing Person. But Olivia, her other daughter, showed her how to check someone's voice messages if she could break the password. For her passwords, Christine always used the street address from their derelict little split-level on the south side of Ann Arbor, the one where Lynette had spent many good hours teaching Christine in preparation for kindergarten.

Olivia brought Lynette a vodka and cranberry and one for herself. They sat on Olivia's pink floral sofa, listening to Christine's messages on speaker phone while Olivia's boy Henry ran plastic farm animals violently into each other. Wet explosions punctuated Christine's messages, which included the latest hysteria from Lynette, "Hello? Hello? Are you alive, this is your MOTHER," an inquiry about a puppy Christine had apparently found and postered for in her neighborhood, and a litany from a man comparing Christine's body parts to various food and drink: her mouth was orange soda. Her calf was a smooth, curved eggplant.

If Christine was alive, why would she stop speaking to her mother? Perhaps there had been a car accident involving Christine and a large tree in a deep wood. When she came to, the bumper was only slightly damaged and she assumed nothing was wrong, but really she had upset her brain, causing her to lose a small square of memory, the square containing her mother.

"I was a good mother," Lynette told Olivia.

Olivia shrugged, frowning at her son, who solemnly piled all his farm animals into what looked like a mass grave on the deep pink rug. Only the pig lived. The pig spoke through Henry. "Dear Heavenly Father!" it bellowed.

"There's so many sitcoms today," Olivia said. "It's hard to tell the difference between good and tragically funny."

Olivia's living room was a woman exploded: everything pink and red and cream, which could've been surprising given Olivia was the only female in the house. But once she became a stay-at-home, Olivia seemed intent on claiming the domestic space for herself, and nobody bothered convincing her there was some real guts-and-gore to the place. When Lynette first saw the room redone, she said to her daughter, "I didn't know you were a girl!" Olivia sniffed and said, "You always deprived me of pink."

But at least she hadn't stopped talking to her.

"I'm still her mother," Lynette said. "Maybe you could tell me why she won't call her own mother."

"She thinks you try too hard and it's depressing."

Henry ran full speed toward the couch and scrambled onto his mother's lap. His pig traversed the loose midsection of Olivia's purple sweater and then climbed the steep incline of her arm.

"What does that mean?" Lynette asked. "She told you that?"

"Sometime, I think. She won't speak to me anymore, either. We argued over circumcision, about which she knows absolutely nothing."

The pig reached Olivia's shoulder and jumped. It flew through the air and plopped into Lynette's half-full glass.

"Thank you," Lynette said. They watched the pig sink to the bottom. "I was hoping he'd do that."

"He's a bad pig," Henry said.

"What's bad about him?" Olivia asked.

"He's a faker."

"It's not the worst thing." Olivia sighed. She told Lynette, "That's how his father describes our neighbor. She's a bubbly person. She literally shrieks when she sees Henry."

"Your father can't appreciate enthusiasm." Lynette set her drink on the coffee table and fished for the pig. "He'd like to squash it out of the world."

"Squash," Henry said, pushing his palm against his mother's thigh.

"Maybe I'll take a drive to Cleveland and see about Christine."

"You should call first." Olivia took hold of Henry's wrist. "Stop that. Leave a message."

Henry let out a yelp and then another. He twisted his body. He kicked Olivia's shin.

Lynette took hold of the boy's ankles, and she and Olivia stretched him on the couch and held him down as he writhed. "Do you know anything about sacrifice?" Lynette asked him. She couldn't stand the boy sometimes. They let him run around like a wild boar tearing up lettuce.

Henry yelped some more and then launched into full-fledged wails. Christine's nose was a red seedless grape. The man had said it. Her butt was two halves of a plum.

"I won't leave her a message," Lynette told Olivia over the screams. "I won't give her a chance."

—ɯ—

Henry and Olivia fell asleep, curled together on the couch, while Lynette grew sleepy in the recliner, looking at the abstract drippings her daughter called artwork, the nicks in the wall still apparent beneath the fresh red paint. The house was comfortable enough, but she couldn't tell if her daughter was a success, or if success could be measured in the way Lynette wanted. Take all the daughters in the world. How did her own compare? Lynette wouldn't live forever and before she died she wanted to know, what could she have done? What was her fault?

Olivia and Henry slept through the ruckus Olivia's husband made in the entryway. He walked into the living room in his old brown slippers; his feet looked deflated in them, and the dirt-stained laces flung against the floor.

"You staying for dinner?" he asked.

"I don't have the energy."

He frowned at his wife and son on the couch. "What'd you do to them?"

She struggled to lift herself from the chair. "I wish you'd buy some new slippers."

"You do?" he asked. "That's why I keep them."

His black SUV was still warm. Gray slush formed a wavy line against the curb, and clumps of muddy snow covered the lawns. The husband watched Lynette adjust the vents. She traced the dusty dash with her finger. In labor, the nurses had made her rate her level of pain. Three you're still smiling. Five is a grimace. Eight and you can't even open your eyes.

"Do you think Olivia's a success?" Lynette asked. "Give her a number, on a scale from one to ten." She pulled her lips back in a grimace. "I've heard if you smile a lot you're a success. But I never trusted that kind of measurement." She watched herself in the side-mirror, hating the man on Christine's voice message. Her daughter's heart was a cup of hot chocolate. Her lungs were two hot-pockets. Ham and cheese.

"I'm sleeping with someone in my office," the husband said. "I can't tell Olivia. I can't stop fucking the woman." He pulled to a stoplight. Lynette felt the vehicle's vibrations in her cheeks.

"Are you going to tell her?" he asked.

Lynette didn't want to know about this. Olivia wouldn't either. "She'd feel bad about it."

"Seems like the kind of information a mother would get across best."

She wanted her daughters to be good and proud and happy. She wanted them to love and trust that she was a good mother. "I'd rather she believe she has a happy life."

He pulled into her driveway in Appleridge. It was a community for retired people. Tired and then retired, like old food dried out and zapped in the microwave.

He leaned his head against the steering wheel. "Nobody's happy."

"Sure we are." Her girls were in pieces. They didn't belong to her anymore. "Watch us smile."

—◊◊◊—

A couple of years ago, Lynette had her license taken away for driving under the influence. She'd crashed into the large painted rock at the edge of the University of Michigan's campus; she was trying to read what it said. "Give it back Lynette!" it looked like. When she returned to examine the words in the morning, however, the message had already been painted over by some kids promoting a Jungle Animal Party.

She always used the same cab driver, a smoker with short hair and a thick groomed beard. He was nice to her, which was a change from most people. He noticed bright things about the day: the briskness, a clean spot of snow, and they appreciated them together.

He agreed to drive Lynette to Cleveland on his day off. Olivia decided to ride with them. She brought Henry, carried him draped over her arm like a piece of luggage. Prone to car sickness, Henry took the window seat opposite Lynette, scrambled onto his knees, and pressed his mouth against the glass.

"Everyone comfortable and happy?" the driver asked.

"Thanks for asking," Lynette said. "We're wonderful." Life could be simple for her and the driver. They were of the same mind.

"I need a vacation," Olivia said. On the bench between Lynette and Henry, she opened her purse and placed several tiny bottles of peach and mint schnapps in her lap. It wasn't an option for Olivia to drive them; Lynette would never allow it, given that her daughter was a lush. She liked having the driver along, anyway. He hummed pleasantly.

Olivia wore large black sunglasses and her hair in a cream silk scarf. She had a bruise on her right temple.

"Is that from the husband or the boy?" Lynette asked.

Henry screeched softly and fogged the glass.

"It's like living in a washing machine," Olivia said.

There was a way Lynette could have her daughter back. But the boy would come too, and the outcome wouldn't be any good. It would be Lynette's fault. The three of them in the apartment where retired people went to die.

The driver lit a cigarette. Lynette rolled down her window and crossed her arms, and the driver seeing her turned up the heat. He didn't put out his cigarette, but he was a nice man.

"What if I was pregnant?" Olivia whispered, looking at her shimmery white coat. She offered Lynette one of the small schnapps bottles.

"I was a single mother," Lynette said to Olivia, loud enough for her driver to hear.

"Very brave," he said between puffs.

"We handled our own selves," Olivia said. "I could do it if I had myself as a daughter."

"You have a poor memory." Lynette nearly gagged on the schnapps. She took a long swallow.

"Crying is a coping mechanism," Olivia said. "It doesn't mean I need anyone." She frowned at Lynette and cried, little hiccups, into the collar of her coat.

Lynette watched the driver's smoke swept up by the wind. She couldn't think about Olivia right now. She had another daughter who wouldn't even speak to her.

"I used to encourage my daughter Christine to act like a monkey," she said. "Up and down the cereal aisle. I'd tell people she had a rare banana disorder."

The driver nodded. "You were a good mother." He glanced at Olivia in the rearview mirror.

"We'll see how your sister's living," Lynette told Olivia. She had no intention of begging Christine to speak with her. She would show up and say, "Who could shut the door on her own mother?"

Olivia sniffed. "What kind of animal did I pretend to be?"

"You were crazy about cheese," Lynette said.

They crossed into Ohio. Henry lunged for his mother's midsection and clung. This was Lynette's family. This was what became of what she had made. Give them food. Give them money. She couldn't stand looking at them. They belonged on a city street, shivering.

Lynette counted the snow-draped farmhouses they passed on the highway. This kind of spaced apart living might have been preferable. They could've plowed their own street and dug out the car and built a whole army of snowmen to protect them instead of stealing from the neighbors' yards to make one dwarfish man with a lopsided head.

"Is she okay?" the driver asked.

Olivia whimpered. She leaned against her son, sipping schnapps.

What had the man called Christine's elbows? Carrot sticks. Her skin as smooth as processed cheese.

"Ever since my husband died," Lynette told the driver, "this family has enjoyed crying." That was the cost of having people around. Her dead husband's sturdy friends who took the girls to steak and reminded them. The ones who stayed with Lynette and were there in the morning. The neighbors with their shared pot-roasts and extra presents at the holidays: those porcelain clowns, one superior to the one with a chipped earlobe.

The girls had fought their whole lives. They wanted affection or some special thing more than the other had. When they fought with those porcelain clowns, they broke them; they tangled and rolled in cracked clown bits. The girls' faces red and tear-streaked gazing from the entryway closet didn't stop Lynette from closing the door, and she locked it. Days later, they still hurt. Days later, Lynette found smooth white pieces embedded in the girls' thighs.

—◊◊◊—

"Ladies, we're here," the driver said.

Christine's yellow-brick townhouse stood bright against the snow. Two snow-filled terracotta pots sat on the steps, and a green bike tethered to the handrail had its front tire capped with white.

"She hasn't been riding," Lynette said.

Olivia moaned and stirred beside her. "It's dangerous in the snow." She rested her chin on Lynette's shoulder. "You can't see what's beneath."

"Christine likes that sort of thing," Lynette said.

From the front seat, Henry peered at them. His blond hair was twisted into two messy horns. "Time for blood milk." His pig sat on the dashboard facing the driver.

"You mean strawberry," Olivia said. "It's not time for that."

Lynette had forgotten what she was going to say. She would knock on the door. She would wait. "Maybe I should tell her I have an illness. Not cancer or anything. She'd never believe it."

"Tell her you have a cold," Olivia said.

"I want blood milk."

Lynette let herself out of the van. Her legs were numb. She wore all black: dress, pearls, heels, coat, wanting to look somber and apologetic, but now she wished she had something sunny on. She stumbled over the curb before reclaiming herself. Olivia stepped beside her and took her arm.

"Poor Mother," she said. "The cancer named Christine has claimed her heart."

The driver watched them. He smiled. He was almost her friend.

"Will you wait for us?" Lynette asked.

He gave her a thumbs-up and took out a cigarette. Behind him, Henry screeched.

"Don't start anything," she told her daughter, who went to the passenger side and gathered her son.

"About my choice to raise a civilized penis? At least not until you've had your say."

Henry's screeches graduated to long, high-pitched wails. There were no tears involved. He flew his pig and cow around his mother's head, through her hair, into her ear. Olivia rang the doorbell, her back angled steeply to accommodate the flailing boy.

Lynette held her hand over the peephole so Christine wouldn't see them. With her free hand, she pulled Henry's ankle. "Why do you like strawberry milk? Do you want to be a little girl?"

She nearly flew forward. In the doorway stood a tall man wearing green pajama pants. His chest was moderately hairy.

"You must be the one eating up my daughter," Lynette said. Her daughter was a pile of food.

"Possibly." The man looked at Henry, who had placed his animals on top of his mother's head.

"We heard your voice message," Lynette said. "It wasn't original."

The man laughed. "I didn't know the line was tapped."

"Next time you should compare her to a wobbly lamp," Olivia said. She shook her head and the animals fell.

"Blood! Milk!" shrieked Henry.

The man let them inside. He pinched Henry's leg, and Henry stopped screaming. He stared at the man.

"Pudding?" the man called toward the stairwell. "Little Dumpling?" The man winked at them.

"Bastard!" Christine yelled. She ran into the hallway in a lace nightgown, wielding a ballet slipper above her head. Her curly hair frizzed around her. Her stomach bulged.

"Wait!" the man said. "That's my favorite foot!"

Christine was pregnant. When she saw them, she set the slipper on the wood banister and tucked her left ankle behind her right. "Hello, Mother."

"Good morning little monkey," Lynette said, pulling her top coat button. She felt close to tears. Crying might have helped, but once she thought about it she couldn't begin.

"I'm now referred to as Pudding," Christine said.

"Your sister wanted to apologize," Lynette said. "Also, I might be sick."

"Dumpling, you're a bit see-through," the man said.

Christine put on the single slipper and sway-stepped to the bedroom.

"She hates food names," the man said. "I do it to bug her." He was a beast. Lynette was proud of her daughter with the slipper.

Henry wrapped his arms around his mother's neck and buried his face. "My friends, Mommy."

Olivia pulled two plastic pieces from her coat pocket. A horse. A duck. "I'm not here to apologize," Olivia said as the man led them into a small, bright kitchen. It had been redone, with cupboards to the ceiling and stainless steel pots above the stainless steel sink and the counters clean and white. It seemed to Lynette more laboratory than kitchen. The man walked shirtless and hairy.

"If it's a boy," Olivia said. "Make sure you circumcise him."

"No offense," the man said. "But that's barbaric."

"It's for cleanliness," Olivia said. "And tradition."

Lynette squeezed her daughter's forearm. She didn't know which was less civilized, but she didn't want to hear about it. It was a violence that didn't concern her.

"Alright," Olivia said. "But it's important."

They sat at the table. On the floor beside Lynette were two red bowls, one empty and one filled with dog food so dried out it looked plastic. She didn't think her daughter would save some poor lost creature, but here was the evidence. From Olivia's lap, Henry lunged toward the table and galloped his animals across it.

"Do you think Christine's a success?" Lynette asked the man. "On a scale from one to ten."

"It depends on the scale." The man went to the counter.

In front of Lynette, the horse lay on its side. The duck hovered over it. "Dear Heavenly Father!" Henry slammed the duck onto the horse so it skidded across the table. This was the problem with the boy. He had nice little animals and he was ferocious with them.

"I know it's a judgment," Lynette said. It was too early to ask for a drink. She'd had the schnapps at least.

The man took his time measuring coffee. "I'd give her a nine-point-five."

Olivia snorted.

"That's not good enough," Christine said, entering the kitchen. She'd put on a robe, but she didn't tie it. She was different from the daughter Lynette remembered, the school pictures she'd tucked inside her desk drawer with important papers. Christine's nipples were wide smudges beneath her nightgown.

"Nine-point-five is a good number," Lynette told her. "I'd feel good about it."

"Just wait until you have the kid," Olivia said. "Nobody's good as a mother."

Lynette frowned. "Don't say that." At least she'd gotten herself into the house. At least they were having a conversation.

"There's no such thing," Olivia said, "as a good mother."

"We'll see," Christine said.

Henry slammed his animals on the table. "Pink! Milk!"

Christine held her hand toward Henry. "I'm your aunt. They tell you about me?"

Henry's hands froze above his animals.

"You've met Auntie before," Olivia said. "Say hello like a human."

Henry turned toward his mother's chest. Olivia tried to turn his head back around, but he cried and flailed against her.

"You should be ashamed," Lynette told Christine. "Living like a missing person with your lost dogs and your nephew's a stranger."

The man belonging to Christine barked twice and howled. He made a clattering getting the mugs down from the cupboard.

"No wonder you can't hear the phone," Lynette said.

Christine sat beside Lynette and propped her feet on a chair. "I heard it." She placed her hands on her stomach. "Do you like the kitchen, mother? We've redone everything. I'm an executive now."

"It's a nice place for a little monkey to dirty up." Lynette had a feeling she shouldn't have come. She would've liked to be part of a family. She would've liked to be treated like a good mother.

On the table, a cow and a sheep lay on their sides. "Are they sleeping or dead?" Christine asked Henry. He didn't answer, and Christine looked at Olivia. "Your husband's going at his secretary. He left me a message about it."

Lynette pinched Christine's arm, and Christine let out a howl. Lynette could've killed her. "I don't believe it," Lynette said. "You're good girls and everyone knows it."

"Don't touch me, Mother," Christine said. "Everything you do hurts the baby."

Olivia pulled more animals out of her pocket. She lined them on the table, a dozen, facing Henry. "It's a relief," Olivia said. "Now I've a real excuse to move into the gutter."

Henry grabbed two of the animals and Olivia fought them out of his grip. She returned the animals to a line facing him, and Henry ruined the line, and it was a game between them.

"Don't listen to her," Lynette said. "You've got a happy life." On the way home, Lynette would ask Olivia to live with her. Bring the boy if she needed to. Lynette had lost one daughter, but she'd keep the other.

The coffee machine beeped, and as they sat around the table silent they heard the man humming. He was a civilized beast. Christine stretched her arms toward the ceiling, lifting her stomach. Her breasts rose above it. The man brought the coffee to the table, and Christine took a mug.

"You're not going to drink that," Lynette said.

Henry broke free from Olivia and gathered the animals in a heap. He whimpered.

"I hope you have some red dye," Olivia told the man. She wouldn't look at her sister.

"We've got plenty of it," Christine said.

"You know what caffeine does to a baby?" Lynette asked. She had suffered while pregnant. Her whole life she had given things up.

"Get out of here, Mother."

Lynette watched Christine drink the coffee. She wanted to believe they had good lives, all of them. But there wasn't room for a belief like that. Christine was a monster now. She was bigger than the rest of them. Her breasts were bright green tomatoes. Her stomach was a burgeoning head of broccoli.

The Year We Are Twenty-Three

Our refrigerator makes a lot of noise. It creaks. It cries. It moans and whines. Orange dots cover the bottom of the door and disappear near the handle. No matter where the temperature's set, it's too cold. The vegetables are frosty; our drinks are slushies: orange slushy, Coke slushy, milk slushy.

We are twenty-three and there are certain things we have to deal with.

We live in a duplex and our neighbors play the stereo too loud. They are army punks, meaning they were both in the army and have spiky hair and leather bands around their wrists and many tattoos. The girl has a bumper sticker that says *Good girls get fat, bad girls get eaten.*

Down the street are grad students; around the corner are the projects. On two-foot slabs of cement porches, middle-aged men sit in chairs pushed flat against brick walls, and they drink beer and watch as I walk by. Sometimes they yell things. It's hard to know whether to look at them or not. I'd never tell anyone this, but they make me nervous. I don't know how to handle it.

I've heard this story: two blocks from those projects, at the corner of Division and Liberty, a man once climbed on top of a roof and shot people as they walked by. I walk by this corner every day on my way to work. There are two kinds of people who live in this city. There are students and there are crazy people.

I live with a boy and we are not married. We are unlikely to get married anytime soon, and I'm sorry if people have a problem with that—really, I am. We have a good understanding of each other, and here's an example. One morning a few months ago, I went into the kitchen for my handful of granola and glass of milk. The gym where I work opens at 5:00 a.m. and I'm the morning girl, so it was still pitch dark and I was groggy from sleep when I flipped on the light and stumbled toward the counter and saw two cockroaches together on the linoleum floor. Their back ends were pushed against each other, their flat heads and stringy antennas pointed in opposite directions. I screamed, "Cedric!" That's all I could say, "Cedric!"

It took a few seconds, but Cedric came running out in his boxers, all skinny legs and long arms and blinking eyes and hair all over the place. And bare feet. I pointed to the cockroaches. They were wiggling around, really getting going, and Cedric stopped short and stared. The refrigerator wailed like a man in a nightmare.

Before I knew it Cedric had the RAID out from beneath the sink and pointed inches above the spot of copulation, filling the room with the sweet smell of chemical death. Both cock-roaches tried to run away, but they were stuck together. They could see freedom ahead of them, but something was holding them back!

Cedric said, "Bring me a shoe! Quick!" We were both in tears by then, from the RAID and from bearing witness to such unimaginable suffering. Afterward we collapsed on the couch. The cockroaches had been swept into the yellow dustbin and covered with two precious sheets of paper towel. Cedric took my hand and curled up around it. He held my hand close to the sunken-in part of his chest. His heart pounded like a jackrabbit. We didn't have sex for a month after that.

—ᘯᘯᘯ—

At the duplex, we have stacks of books all over the place. That's what we do when we clean. We pull the books scattered around the floor, from the countertops, kitchen table, coffee table, and couch, and we pile them into stacks that reach our knees. Sometimes we push these stacks against the wall; sometimes we leave them in the middle of the living room. Think what could happen if it goes on much longer: we will be living among hundreds of pillars of books. We will sit on one stack to look through the contents of another. We will weave through them to move from the kitchen to the bedroom. But we can't help it; these are our remains. We are no longer students. We are no longer students.

* —◊◊◊—

Cedric has started a new job at a grocery store and works every day from 2:00 to 10:00 p.m. I work every day from 5:00 a.m. to 2:00 p.m., and this leaves a small window nightly during which, when we're able to stop thinking about the roaches long enough, we sometimes have sex. To keep the romance alive we have agreed to leave notes every day on the refrigerator for each other, and here, roughly, are the rules. The idea is to not think about what we are writing but to just write it, with the mutual understanding that we are trying out ideas and seeing if they make any sense. The most exciting cases will be when something doesn't make any sense to the one who wrote it but makes perfect sense to the one who reads it.

My first one to Cedric said this: If someone listens to loud music all the time, their brain becomes an empty sound cave and when the music stops they die.

The first one from Cedric said this: There are tiny birds that live in our stomachs and they are always hungry!

Work for me is the gym, and lately there is a problem. I try hard not to judge people, but there are two types of gym-goers, and believe it or not these people are all over the place: conservatives and liberals.

Lately there is a war. The liberals have always walked around naked in the locker room. The conservatives have always changed in stalls behind long mildewed curtains and then stood around the gym giving shocked looks and talking about the liberals. This has been going on for a while, but now the liberals are growing bolder. They are leaving their clothes in piles in the locker room. They are walking around the gym naked and they are using the machines.

The conservatives are more energized. They walk around in big strides with their eyes wide open, and they stand by my counter and whisper, because when conservatives are angry they yell in soft voices, and they'll spit on your arm if you leave it in range. They whisper, "Do something about it! Make them stop! Kick them out! We were here first!"

They all disappear by 9:00 a.m., a full hour before the owner comes in, and since I've worked the morning shift the past four months and the walking around naked is a newish phenomenon, the owner would at first hear nothing about it. He would not even look at me. While flipping through his Rolodex, he said, "Until ten o'clock, dearie, you're in charge, and if you can't deal with them I'll find someone else who can."

—〰—

The gym smells rubbery and metallic early in the morning, and the equipment shines: white and black and dark red. Seeing all those empty machines and the thousands reflected in the mirrors makes my muscles itch. Four months ago, I didn't even know what a bench press was.

I inspect the cleaning job of the night manager. I wrap my ankles around the sit-up bar for a quick set of twenty-five, and by the time I get to twenty I see Sidney waiting outside the door in a ridiculous coat, all puffy and gray. *Twenty-one*, Sidney. *Twenty-two*, Sidney. She's watching me.

"How's it going," I say. I swing the door open and pop the side-locks into place. "Another beautiful morning." The only good thing about winter mornings in Michigan is that you can believe for a second the day might turn out bright and sunny and beautiful.

Sidney signs in and says, "When are you going to do something about those nudists?"

Just as she's saying this, one walks in, a high-waisted, white-haired lady with a fat bottom and huge calves. She says hello to me, politely, and says nothing to Sidney. Five minutes later she's doing leg lifts in the nude, and Sidney stares at me, her face bright red.

Another half hour and I'm in the middle of a battle zone: the nakeds on one side, the clothed on the other, every one of them with their backs to each other, staring in the mirror and keeping track of their enemies. There is a line. The clothed have no access to the weights. The nakeds have no access to the aerobic machines.

I spend the morning staring mainly at the liberals. They start off pale, but their whole bodies turn pink as they strain to do their lifts and weights and presses. Many of them are overweight and that is a lot of skin to see every day. Most mornings it's enough to make me get from behind the counter and climb onto an exercise bike. Most mornings I ride along with the conservatives.

I write on the refrigerator: Someday I'm going to be terrifically fat and suffer along with everyone else.

Cedric writes: There is suffering in this world, but you don't have to see it unless it's on the floor having sex in front of you.

The next day when the nudists leave and my boss gets in, I explain to him the seriousness of the situation. About them sitting on the machines. About their skin red from rubbing against the foam rubber. "This isn't sanitary. The health team will come and write stories about this place. Nudists will come from all over the country. It will be a nudist colony."

He turns his head at this and looks concerned. "You need to tell them to stop. I'm not joking around."

—∿—

That night I am still awake when Cedric gets home, and he comes to sit with me on the couch. I tell him about the nudists. I have to yell because of the music next door.

He says, "Suddenly the gym seems like an interesting place to be."

I say, "Seriously, what am I going to do?"

The bass line pulses through the wall like an unstoppable maniac pounding at the door. It changes the chemistry in the room. The top books on our stacks shake. In seconds the whole place could fall apart.

Cedric says, "I guess you'll have to say something to them."

"What am I supposed to say?"

"Just tell them your boss was born in the Stone Age and can't handle their free spirits leaving wet spots all over his equipment."

Cedric does not fully understand about the liberals. Like I said, they are hard to look at and hard not to look at. They are a lot of old naked bodies all together. They are a lot of skin and a lot of wrinkles and rolls, and I don't know where to rest my eyes when I talk to them. Every time I open my mouth, they smirk, daring me to say something. The liberals are fewer, but they are stronger than their enemy, and they are not easily going to let go of their freedom.

Cedric looks at me for an answer. His eyes are puffy and bloodshot, and I see he's gotten even skinnier in the arms and around the neck. His veins are thick and blue. He looks like he just shot up or found out someone died. I crawl onto his lap and take off his shirt. His ribs poke out like sticks under a blanket. I run my fingers along them. We have sex on the couch in time to the music.

Afterward I tell him, "You need to eat more."

He says, "You like me like this."

I close my eyes. We are on opposite ends of the couch with our legs stretched beside each other. I say, "Too bad for the owner. I'm not saying anything to those liberals."

Sidney is waiting for me when I get to work the next morning.

"We don't open till five," I say.

She says she has something to tell me. The conservatives are planning a rebellion. They will steal all the piles of clothes from the locker room while the liberals are working out.

"You think they're going to care?" I ask. "They'll have an excuse to go outside like that all day."

"It's freezing!" Sidney says. "Trust me. They'll care."

By six o'clock everyone is on their own side studying each other in the mirrors. I study the nudes. I look at the women's breasts and the men's lower areas and watch them shake or shrivel and turn purple and bruised. I can't help it. I am disgusted and fascinated by this torturing of their bodies.

The sit-up bar is on the liberal side of the room, and sometimes, when I've stared long enough at enough flabby stomachs, I have an urge to tone my abs. I am the only clothed person who crosses to the other side. The nudes look at me until satisfied I am not going to say anything. They tolerate me because they have to and because, although I stare, I never give them dirty looks.

I'm halfway through my first set of sit-ups when, upside down, I glimpse the conservatives grouping together. *Fifteen. Sixteen.* The nudes set down their weights and watch them in the mirrors. *Seventeen. Eighteen.* Sidney and a thin woman in glasses rush to the locker room. *Nineteen. Twenty.* The nudes look at each other. *Twenty-one. Twenty-two.* Sidney and the woman run out of the locker room, each with a bulky black garbage bag in her arms. *Twenty-three. Twenty-four.* Their faces are grim and serious. *Twenty-five.* Upside down, I watch along with the nudes as the two clothed women run to the door.

The nudes look at me as I stand and fix my ponytail. A few walk hesitantly toward the locker room. The rest of the conservatives grab their bags and head for the door. In minutes there will be chaos.

On the refrigerator I write: The conservatives steal the clothes; the liberals steal the towels. Things will never change.

Cedric writes: We are all of us exposed.

—\/\/\—

I am home alone all day with nothing to do, and sometimes I go searching and sometimes I find things. In a box in the bedroom at the bottom of a dozen pictures, I find a picture of Cedric from high school. He is there with his family, in the middle, with his arms around his mother and younger brother, except it doesn't look like him because he is fat. He is not smiling in the picture. With his arms and shoulders raised, a thin moon of stomach hangs over his jeans. I sit on the bed and look at the picture a long time.

On the refrigerator I write: I don't know what I'm searching for.

Cedric writes: Search for me.

—\/\/\—

Tension is high at the gym. There are two types of people in this world: those who walk around naked and those who hate them.

Sidney is a hero on the conservative side. She looks younger. There is a small grin on her face. She works the Stairmaster like she's never worked it before. When she's done, she looks directly at the liberal side. She grabs her water bottle and walks to the leg press, a currently liberal-owned machine. The liberals turn from the mirror and watch her. The conservatives turn around and watch her, too. The grin on Sidney's face is bigger, but she's not looking at anyone. She doesn't look triumphant: her eyes are too blurry. She is somewhere peaceful. She is happy.

The liberals watch her for a while, and then one nudges another, and the two of them cross to the conservative side and get on the treadmills. In a few seconds they have those grins on their faces, too. For a minute I think maybe the world is something more complex than I thought. For that minute I think I am only twenty-three and know nothing about people and their motivations.

But all at once the liberals pass to the conservative side and the conservatives to the liberal. They climb onto their machines and turn carefully away from each other to look in the mirrors, and once more in the mirrors there are thousands of them.

The conservatives work their quads and calves and biceps. The liberals work the bikes and treadmills and Stairmasters. The line is drawn again.

—⚒—

At 10:30 I stop Cedric at the door and point to the car. We get in and it's hot from him driving. It's like stepping into an oven. I take him to Denny's and order two burgers. I shove mine in my mouth and take huge bites and barely chew. I can't swallow fast enough.

I'm halfway through mine when I look at Cedric. He hasn't touched his burger. His collarbone sticks out, thick and pale between the red peaks of his shirt. "Eat. Eat," I tell him.

He squints at the burger and screws up his face, like he sees two cockroaches dying in front of him. "What's the problem?" he asks.

I start to cry. "What's the problem?" I want to say something else but I can't say anything. I can't say anything. In the Denny's bathroom with my head against the toilet rim, I throw up for three minutes.

On the refrigerator I write: The world is full of black and white and there are only two ways to look at it: the right way and the wrong way.

Cedric writes: The refrigerator was wailing when we came to this place, and it will be wailing when we leave.

I write: We are not crazy people.

He writes: If you look at it the right way.

Put the Animals to Bed

The little boy said they were brothers. The aunt—never before a brother—was pleased. The boy had her sister's light blonde hair. He held the aunt's hand the moment she arrived, pulled her to the floor with his collection of horses and cowboys and various ranch fixings. Among the brown and gray horses were two pink ponies with sparkly blonde manes.

"You run the Dude Ranch," the boy told the aunt. He pointed to a shoebox turned over. The pink ponies approached—they had very deep voices. "We're not from 'round these parts."

"Please," the aunt said. "Stay here."

She and the boy held hands while the other horses galloped over and asked for admittance. The aunt's job was to lift and lower the shoebox while the boy toddled the horses inside. The boy's father watched from the couch, cradling a green glass pipe. Even the porch had smelled of marijuana. Once, he and the aunt had smelled this way together.

"You still look like a human," the father told the aunt.

The boy squeezed her hand. "This is my brother," the boy said.

"Hey buddy, do you know what a brother is?" asked the father.

The boy didn't answer. When all the horses were inside, the boy let go of her hand and fell back on the carpet. "Bed now, please." He blinked at the ceiling. His bare feet twitched.

The father carried him thrown over his shoulder. "Say good-night to Auntie."

"Goodnight, Brother," the boy said.

The aunt pulled a package of airline pretzels from her jacket. In a room above her, the boy cried. She ate the pretzels in quick bites, then licked the salty package. Three years ago, she'd seen the boy. Her sister had sent a picture of herself with the baby, pushing him toward the camera like an offering. The aunt had almost returned then.

The boy's father joined her on the floor with a digital camera. He was a deadened version of her friend from high school—his eyes sagged, his beard dirty. He showed what she had missed: her sister's white casket, a hearse, a carved-out cemetery plot.

"Delete," he said. "Delete." As they went, he erased each picture.

"I'm glad I missed it," the aunt said.

"You weren't friends."

"That's not why I'm glad."

She asked for a glass of water and they went into the kitchen. Her legs ached from the plane ride and then the taxi. She'd shared with a man who lived a few neighborhoods over; upon arrival, she'd shouted, "Anyone heading to the south side?" The man told her about his mother organizing blind dates he didn't show up for. "Even when things work out they don't really work," the man said. He wore a coat two sizes too large. He ducked his head often toward his left shoulder. He must've known they were the same—friendless.

In the kitchen, the tap water was warm. The boy's father apologized but didn't seem sorry. The floor was covered with food bits. The room was dim—bulbs missed.

"Excuse us," he said. "We live very close to death."

"You should move." She drank her whole glass of water.

"It'd sneak in the trunk at the last minute." He poured himself a glass of milk and drizzled in chocolate syrup. In the airplane bathroom—to avoid emotional suicide with the father—the aunt had twice masturbated. She told this to the dateless man in the taxi. "Any emotion is suicide," the man said.

The father poured half his chocolate milk into her glass. "I've considered making the boy stay up past his bedtime."

"That baby's no longer a baby."

"He still eats with miniature forks," said the father. "He puts all his toys to sleep before bed."

The aunt drank the chocolate milk: her sister's drink for when she felt less than human. Humans were social creatures. They gathered around others and reached out for others and formed groups they named Family. Friends. Outsiders. The aunt planned to stay the weekend, take the boy to the aquarium, rest her face against the glass and encourage him to do the same. She planned to miss her sister this way—a missed mother.

Above them, the boy cried. The father excused himself and the aunt drank the rest of her milk and also the father's. She cleaned the glasses with too much dish soap and scalding water. The man in the taxi had a nephew as well, but no children of his own. He believed they would be crippling.

With his sweet marijuana breath, the father returned and stood beside her. They watched her hands redden in the water.

"He wants his brother." The father turned off the sink. "Careful with him. He's already given up on female toys."

In his room, the boy stood beside a small plastic desk. "It's okay." He stroked the edge of the desk. "Shhhh. I'll see you tomorrow. Shhhh." He swayed, shushing the desk, and then he raised his hands to his head. "Why won't you sleep!"

"I'll help," the aunt said. She led the boy to bed and straightened the covers across his chest. He watched as she paced the room, as she pet each object and offered comfort. "Sweet dreams," she told the clock. "It'll be alright."

When all was asleep, she left the boy's room and in the living room found a pillow and a blanket on the couch. She lay down in her clothes and pulled the blanket tight around her and immediately slept. She woke a little later.

A weak voice in the room: "Can I sleep with you, Brother?"

"Please," she told the boy. "Stay here."

March On

Mired in the late processes of moving, my mother left trails of things everywhere: clothes strewn from dressers, condiments rolling by the refrigerator, stacks of books leading from shelves in ragged, precarious steps. I hadn't realized these things were left: they'd been so well hidden in drawers, behind doors, in tight-lines of themselves; but now they were dragged out and dropped, abandoned as my mother flitted around, suddenly overwhelmed, suddenly needing help.

"Clutter." She fluttered her hands toward the boxes she'd sealed weeks ago. "It's like that tricky triangle. People get lost."

She called a few moving companies, asked if they had any women movers, then ranted about discrimination and division of labor. They hung up, and she stared at the phone incredulously. She walked to something heavy and yelled for me to grab the camera. "Look at me!" she said, her arms struggling to embrace the microwave a foot above the counter. We took pictures of her lifting things, and then I guess she sent them to the moving companies with slews of hateful exclamations.

"I don't want any strange men," she said. "I don't deal well with strange men." She stared at my skinny arms. "You could be the first woman mover in Chapel Hill." She sighed and asked for Sid's number, the high school dropout who'd hung around the house off and on since last summer.

"Sid's a strange man," I said. "Emphasis on strange."

"He's a boy," she said. "That's different."

The next morning, I got ready for school when a truck rumbled up to the house. The engine shuddered off and these insanely happy voices emerged: you could tell by the tones, the great inflections, though they said things like, "My limbs feel like rubber in the morning" and "Look at the dew on the grass, man! I never get to see that shit."

The front door opened and everyone yelled hello like they arrived at some rowdy party. Mom told them there was coffee in the kitchen. Convenient for her to think of Sid as a boy at eighteen, while she called me, at sixteen, a woman. Titles like that could be confusing. They implied a level of capability, a willingness to endure awkwardness for the "greatest good" of the family.

"I'm going to say hi to Raimy," Sid said, and I fumbled with the last buttons of my blouse. He bounded up the stairs. "Excuse me." He panted. He wore a ribbed tank-top and huge jeans and his frizzy hair in a knot. "Would you like to purchase a trip to Madman Island?"

"What's playing this week?"

He smiled at me, all dressed up. "The Banker and the Bum."

"I've seen it too many times."

"Except this time the bum has a job."

I backed him into the hallway. "It's a prostitute situation. My mom paying you. You being here for money."

"I'm an innocent in all this."

"What's your definition of that?"

"You don't understand how the world works," he told me, going down the stairs. "You keep trying to get away, but here I am."

"The world wants me crazy," I said.

He shrugged and grinned. "Well, it's fate."

—◊◊◊—

Originally, Mom had this idea about fleeing, moving everything at once and never seeing our house again: just get it all out, get it over with. Only she hadn't considered the effect of moving from one big mess to another, with stacks of boxes against new walls and old furniture angled oddly and everything in all the wrong rooms and strewn around the floor and in great troublesome piles. So she developed the philosophy of "one box at a time," of creating an established, serene world to move into: close the door on this one and become a new woman, a relaxed woman, one comfortable again in her own home.

"I can't expect to change like that," she told me and the dropout boys, snapping her fingers; I had coffee with them before school, all of us crowded around the counter since they'd already moved the table. Mom explained how she'd only need the boys in the mornings, but every morning for the next two or three weeks. "It's more satisfying doing it the long way," she said.

"I don't believe in franticism," Sid said. "Or fanaticism?" He grinned at me. "Well, maybe the second one's okay."

I refused to participate. I barely acknowledged what was happening, the long surreal process of restructuring our lives: shifting things over, arranging them differently, like these objects weren't even ours, like they belonged to someone else. I quit going to the new house. I stayed in my room and let everyone know we were saving my things for last.

Dad had already fled my childhood home. He wanted all the details of the move, and I told him about our things on the floor: walked on, kicked at, thrown out of the way. He told me Mom's trying to start a new life. Like him. He motioned vaguely around the room, which wasn't remotely his, not even figuratively: he didn't have a picture frame on the mantle. His "roommate" Rebecca was out of town, and it felt weird being at her place without her, like we'd broken into a random Victorian and waited for the owner to come in and pull out a gun.

"I haven't finished with my first life," I told Dad. "I'm sixteen and forced to start a new one."

"You've had a million lives already," he said. "Every day can be a new life."

"And a new death. If you believe that about every day, there's a lot of dying too."

"I guess I can handle that," he said. "Why not." He held up his glass of milk in a toast, and the ice cubes jangled as our glasses touched like a hundred toasts at once. This was a habit my parents still shared, even now, after who knows how many deaths: they continued to put ice in their drinks. Every night: in water, in soda, in milk; it was a dangerous way of living. Because near the end of the meal, when you parted your lips for that last bit of liquid, the ice flew forward. If you weren't quick enough to re-angle the glass, the cubes crashed into your nose.

—◊◊◊—

"Get out of that war zone," Jenna told me. We sat in the orange vinyl booth of the Chinese restaurant a half-block from the bank I worked in after school. We had a platter of lemon chicken between us.

"There's wreckage all over the place," I said. "It's the whole city. I can't go anywhere. I stagger around."

Jenna nodded. "You're a zombie. It's a form of post-traumatic stress."

"Except it's not really *post*. It's present-traumatic stress." I leaned back in the booth. Constantly, lately, I was eating too much and feeling sick.

"There's no stress in Annapolis." She sorted through the chicken for lemon rinds to suck on. For Spring Break, Jenna wanted to drive to Maryland, and see her boyfriend-of-three-weeks in the Naval Academy. "There's no Sids."

I nodded. We were off Sids. Guys we were in love with along with who knows how many other girls. Guys who believed love was a free spirit and that kind of crap, dating a dozen girls at once and being all good-natured so no one really complained.

I agreed to ride with her. I had a grandmother near there, in Virginia, who sighed and shuffled contentedly around her small cluttered apartment, working on art projects, too focused on the snaps and surges of her own brain to let in much drama.

"Not that I don't want to come and listen to you and James engage in different sorts of combat."

She rolled her eyes. "There's other guys. *Academy* guys."

"Structured guys just pretend reliability better than the bums," I said.

—⁓—

When I got home that night, Mom sat in my bedroom with her glasses on and a pile of paper in her lap. She took time off work for the move, but every day FedEx packages piled by the door. "Don't talk to me," she said. "I'm in so much shit."

She wore a tie-dye shirt-and-shorts combo. It was almost warm: certain days, certain places, that time of year when we turned off the furnace but weren't ready for the air-conditioner, and the air in the house felt stagnant, hanging there, unchanged. Everyone just wanted to be outside. We were waiting for the weather to catch up with that.

I shed my work clothes and put on my pajamas, keeping my back to Mom, feeling self-conscious and thinking it had something to do with Sid.

"Wait," Mom mumbled. "Wait, wait, no."

I lay on my bed and closed my eyes. We spent a lot of time in my room. It was the only livable place in the house. I listened to paper shuffling and her pen scribbling. Then the cool scratch of paper, a thumbnail driven along a crease. A series of crisp folds.

"Dinner time," Mom said. She slouched in the chair with a paper bird in her lap. She pulled the tail and its wings flapped. "It would be nice to skip over things," she said. "It would be nice if things got done but I didn't have to do them."

"That's a lot of life," I said.

"Well, I'd like to skip it." We stared into space until it felt awkward doing that together. "I guess dinner's not going to make itself like it should," Mom said.

The kitchen was empty besides clumps of dust and a few scattered boxes. I was tired of seeing the house sad and torn up and thinking this was how I'd remember it. I leaned against the counter as she sliced into the plastic sleeve of a frozen pizza. "I'm going to Virginia next week," I said. "I'm driving with Jenna."

"Good. I can unpack through dinner." She pulled strands of hair around her face as I told her I'd stay with Grandma, Dad's Mom.

"It's strange," Mom said. "Having people still alive who feel dead. They're basically dead." She leaned against the counter next to me. We half-looked at each other. We had trouble lately not falling into these awkward conversations. We had trouble not feeling extraordinarily sorry for ourselves.

Mom turned the stove to low and held her hands over a burner. She rubbed her hands together and shivered in her summer clothes. "Sid asks questions," she said. "He wants to know what you were like as a kid. He asks which animals are your favorites." She gave me a dreamy look, one etched with irony or disbelief, a tightening of the lips. "Maybe he's in love."

"Sid's in love with everyone," I said.

Mom nodded. "You can't trust people." She turned on the oven light and looked through the little window. "I'll finish the move while you're gone. It'll be a new life when you get home."

—◊—

Dad wanted to meet me in Virginia. "Don't tell your grandmother anything. About anything."

He and Rebecca brought things to the table: plates, salad, and shiny silverware. It was hard not to pout, doing nothing while people did things for you, like they owed you something.

"I wish I could pretend things were normal," I said. "I'd enter some alternate universe in my head where we were happy again."

"We *are* happy, Raimy," Dad said. He smiled at Rebecca. She moved like a butterfly, bright and nervous, flitting around.

"Okay," I said. "Now that you say so."

They sat at the table and served me, with utensils coming from every direction: salad, chicken, peas, bread. I'd driven the short mile to Rebecca's after work, and the three of us still wore our work clothes, making dinner seem official, like some deal in the making.

"I didn't go for Grandma's birthday," Dad said. "Did you wonder why?"

"I didn't think about it," I said. We used to all go together.

"It's been twenty years since I visited alone. I wasn't sure you'd come.

Rebecca looked at her food. Maybe someday, the three of us would go together. I'd sit in the backseat, and up front, the whole way, I'd see Dad and Rebecca.

"I guess we pretend Mom doesn't exist anymore," I said.

"She exists," Rebecca said, and she took a bite of bread.

"Just let me tell Grandma," Dad said. "I'll try to explain it."

"That will be nice," I said. "I'd like an explanation."

—⁓〠⁓—

Jenna and I left on a warm day, with the windows down and the music loud, so we heard the words over the crackling rush of air.

It felt appropriate leaving Chapel Hill among all that noise. I felt numb, dizzy: pleased.

Earlier that morning, Sid had come into my room and collapsed sweaty on the floor—his long hair in damp ringlets, his T-shirt stretched and torn—and my room filled with the smell of him, this mixture like if we were together.

"How can you leave this excitement?" he asked.

I took off my shoes and put them back on. I sat in the armchair across from him. "I'm trying to avoid you."

A wobbly screech came from downstairs: furniture dragged across wood.

"It's no use now," he said. "I know too much about you. I know about turtles."

"Lots of people like turtles."

He shuffled across the floor, and I let him pull me to the floor.

"I'm in your head," he whispered.

"Get out."

He put his hand on my scalp. "In Virginia, you're going to be bored out of your mind."

"I kissed Sid this morning," I told Jenna over the noise, thinking about him in that peaceful way distance provides, like he was something glossy and stuck in the past.

She lowered the music and gave me a look.

"He'll be gone when I get home," I told her. "I'll never see him again."

"He's like a tick, wiggling his way in," she said. "You can't flick him off."

The wind was a relief, screaming in like a third voice, taking up space and time, and we could listen to that. The highway was lined with different layers of life, some trees coming in with intense green, nearly neon, while others remained a shabby dark green, a nearly dead green, with leaves that had survived over the winter and were now trying to pick themselves up again: battered, haggard.

"The point of this trip was to escape," I said. "Now my dad's coming. I'll be part of the interrogations."

"Just come to the academy," Jenna said.

"It'll be worse," I said. "I can't handle happiness."

"Sometimes it seeps in a little."

"I keep thinking it'll happen with Sid, but it's much worse afterward. It's like going to a movie. The maintenance is impossible."

—m—

A few hours later, we pulled into Grandma's assisted-living community: identical red brick buildings with white doors and white-shuttered windows sealed up so we couldn't see inside.

Grandma didn't answer the door. I pounded and rang the bell, then sat in one of her wrought-iron chairs. Time passed, and I pounded again. Jenna watched from her car until I told her to leave. I said it was wonderful sitting in the sun; I would practice meditation and try to figure out all the loveliness of the world: how it worked, where it came from. She looked skeptical, but she was too nervous about her own life to wait any longer.

I called Grandma's phone and heard it ring. I yelled "Grandma! Grandma!" and looked around the empty street like I ruined the peace for everyone with my selfish desire to get inside.

The sun faded and I pulled a sweater from my suitcase and draped it over my arms like a blanket. I couldn't bring myself to put it on like a normal person. I imagined Grandma wearing giant headphones, painting a hundred balls of socks or the angles of her ceiling, blissfully entranced by some new-age spiritual music into which pounding and ringing blurred easily.

Then, briefly, I decided she was dead. I imagined her pale on the floor and me making all this noise, and I felt even more disruptive. I stared at the quiet street, thinking about us all dead in some ways: this distance between people and the everyday sadness that comes with everyday separation, and maybe we constantly grieved each other and our old lives. The only comfort we had was thinking maybe it was like this for everyone, maybe there was a connection in that.

But I decided Grandma probably wasn't really dead, and I got mad again that she wasn't answering the door. She'd seemed overwhelmingly alive on the phone when I told her about my visit. She kept repeating, "It's been so long. So long so long so long."

Around 7:00, my bag vibrated and I pulled out my phone.

"You're bored, aren't you," Sid said.

I studied the building across the street, identical to this one except no one like me sat outside. "I'm working on my inner ugly," I told him. I wanted someone to drive down the road. I wanted someone to come out one of those doors screaming.

"We made a lot of progress today," he said.

"People are too big on progress. Progress is just another word for change."

"Alright," he said. "We made a lot of change today."

I listened to his breathing and pretended I was there, in Chapel Hill. Not with Sid, but with Mom. I pretended I was helping.

"I don't like you being out of town," he said. "I like thinking I can drive over and see you, even if I don't.

I sighed. "Sid. I don't think you should anymore. You're a bad influence."

He was silent for a while. "Raimy, you shouldn't be so resistant. There's fate and I'm sick of dancing around it. You should be here with us."

"Fate isn't a place!" I yelled, no longer caring about disturbing the silence. "It's a state of mind!" I heard creaking inside the apartment. The door opened, and my grandmother peeked out, blinking like she'd just woken up. I turned off my phone.

"Raimy!" she croaked. "You should've knocked!" She wore a nightgown with pale blue ferns, and her wiry gray hair, usually neat and compact against her head, sprung out in places like stretched coil. She held the door open as I struggled into the dark apartment with my suitcase.

"I was nervous about you coming." She wandered through the gray living room stumbling over bits of paper and cardboard and soft-soled shoes scattered around the floor. Canvases with shadowy half-finished collages leaned on furniture or against the wall, and it was strange coming from a temporary mess, because here was a permanent one. And it felt better, knowing people got used to it if they needed to.

Her hand disappeared beneath a few lampshades and fumbled around, and when all of it failed, she went into the hall and flipped on the light. She gathered her nightgown and twisted it in her hands. "I couldn't sleep last night with you coming. So I took some pills. My doctor gave me some."

"It was nice outside," I told her. "I talked to my friend."

"I heard something." She led me to the guest room, which was really just another work room cluttered with art projects and dressers with drawers marked "Things," "Numbers," "Holes," "Uglies." Stacks of canvases, gray with dust, sat on the bed. "Nobody's visited in a while." She looked away; her eyes climbed the walls like she was trying to place herself. She seemed smaller than I remembered, her shoulders drawn in close as though her chest needed protecting. I took the canvases off the bed.

"I don't leave home until someone visits." She pointed at the canvases. "It piles up." She shuffled back into the hall, and I heard water running, the crash of metal-on-metal, the turn of a dial. I considered crawling into the dusty bed but went into the kitchen and watched her fidget around the room: fold towels, put dishes away, remove teabags and place them in cups. I felt myself pouting again, watching her. While I sat there. Useless.

I asked if I could help, but she didn't seem to hear me. She told me about exhibits in D.C.; she pulled newspaper clippings from a drawer and pointed at pictures of artwork with varying levels of enthusiasm. "We'll go when your parents get here."

"It's just Dad," I said. "Mom's not coming."

She dropped the clippings on the table. "Something happened to her." She squeezed her fists, and her soft, wrinkled face paled. "Tell me. Your dad thinks I can't handle it."

"Something happened," I said, and for a moment I enjoyed her horror because it was mine, too.

"What?" Grandma asked. The teapot grumbled behind her. "What? What?" She stared at my face like she was losing sight of me, like we would all disappear if we looked away for a second.

"It's not what you think," I said.

She sat in the chair across from me, seeming to relax as the tea kettle whimpered.

I went over to stop it. "It's nothing like that," I said, pouring the hot water over the tea bags and standing above the steam. I wanted to keep talking about her. I wanted, again and again, to bring Mom back from the dead.

The Good Luck Doll

Claudia's mother sent the doll in a large yellow envelope that was torn at the top and dirt-smeared. The doll looked familiar: squeezable, dressed in overalls with a white lace-collared shirt adorned with the bright, awkward dots and wavy lines of someone unable to hold a marker properly. A girl with two braids chopped off and a brown smear on her cheek. The note said: *You forgot to take your baby with you.*

Claudia made up Steve's king-sized bed and set the doll in the middle, as a joke. She'd moved into the apartment nearly a year ago and still couldn't think of it as hers. Steve carefully chose his articles. "Hand me my remote," "Let's move my dresser closer to my bathroom." Once he'd said, "My front door's sticking again," and Claudia said, "The door might be yours but the stickiness belongs to the landlord." He ignored her and never got the door fixed. Now with the humidity, she came home and banged her shoulder against the sweet spot in the middle.

She used to keep the doll beneath her childhood bed with the dust and spiders. She'd gotten it in her head that a doll beneath you meant good luck. Even though she couldn't sleep some nights knowing her favorite suffered down there, she won the part of Peter Pan in the school play, and the girls no longer chased her beneath the giant climbable tires or shot rubber bands at her knees.

Claudia brushed her teeth in the bathroom when she heard Steve enter the bedroom. His bed squeaked. "Who are *you*?" he asked. From the doorway she saw Steve hold the doll in the air away from his body, his arms straight.

"That's not how you hold her," Claudia said.

"She's ugly," Steve said. "She might have a disease."

"Well, she's mine." She spit in the sink.

Steve brought the doll into the bathroom, cradling it in his arms. He swayed back and forth, watching himself in the mirror. "Am I a prize or what?" he asked. Ever since he asked her to move in, he had become obsessed. He was fifteen years older than she. He hummed lullabies in the shower. He took her temperature in the morning to determine ovulation.

A few months ago, Claudia spent a long time in the bathroom one evening, imagining herself dead in the mirror, a ceremony she performed whenever strangers ignored the smiles she gave them on the street. She lost some color in her cheeks. When Steve banged on the door, she came out looking pale and horrified. "I'm pregnant," she told him.

He backed away. She sat on the couch, and he surrounded her with pillows. He bought a gallon-sized bottle of prenatal vitamins. "Just this many to go!" They joked around again. He made pancakes in the shapes of donkeys and elephants, and they growled while they ate.

For weeks he didn't touch her, and she tied a small pillow against her stomach. But her mother discovered the pillow the last time they went for dinner. She reached beneath Claudia's T-shirt and tossed the pillow onto Steve's lap. "I'm serious about becoming a grandmother." She pointed to the dozen knitted booties lined by the front door. Steve held the stomach pillow for a moment and then set it on the couch.

Every night since, they had sex as if the rougher he got the more torn open and ready her body would be.

Now, Steve apologized to the doll. "I don't mind if you're ugly." He rocked the doll in his arms. He hugged it.

"The doll used to be good luck," Claudia said. "Let's put it beneath the bed and see if we wake up rich."

Steve frowned at her. He threw the doll in the sink, into the glob of her toothpaste. "That's what you'd wish for?" He pushed the shower curtain to one side and then snapped it closed again. He pulled up her shirt and stuffed the doll into the elastic of her shorts. The toothpaste was cold, smeared against her skin.

"Can't you recognize a joke?" she asked. She looked in the mirror and imagined herself swallowed by the insides of a tire.

Later, when Steve moved toward her, he held the doll between them. He wrapped his arms around her and pressed hard with his stomach so the doll stayed, growing sticky with sweat. Claudia wished into the doll that she would become pregnant. She relaxed. Let one of them feel lucky. She was torn open and ready.

In These Times the Home
Is a Tired Place

PART ONE

1. Only one dream the mother remembered: driving, dead bodies on the road, the word PAPER large and black on a billboard. Sometimes she made up different dreams when she woke panicked in the gray morning, imagining an airport chase, a lake drowning—but they weren't really hers, only dreams she believed she should have instead of always the one: driving through death and the urge to pull over.

2. The girl spent a Saturday morning cutting snowflakes from a pile of paper she'd found on her mother's desk. The snowflakes were peppered with sliced negotiations, diamond-pierced words like *child* and *property* and *alimony*, and when the girl finished she strung the flakes together and hung them from her window so they trailed to the berry bush and flapped in the stirred summer wind.

3. Screamed in the kitchen one night. Too many cooks in the saucepan. Too little wine. Granite counters crusted with crushed tomato, sea salt, sausage casing, but no food besides the steaming meal bleeding over the bin. The girl sent to her room—*Now.*

The father's recipes stacked and chopped to pieces and confettied across the tile. Division always makes less unless one was a fraction to begin with. "Divide by me," the father said. "Then we both come out ahead."

4. Over summer break, the girl wanted projects similar to school but better. The babysitter gave cartoon-spelling tests and driveway geology lessons, brought Dickens and Shakespeare from her Sophomore Advanced English. They read aloud, and with special gaits and one arm thrown theatrically, they trailed one another through the long grass, and the babysitter didn't mind the books this time because words weren't meant to be studied, they were meant to be screamed.

5. The mother missed something every night. In the grocery line stretched back to frozen foods, her customer-in-training pushed a full-sized cart in which lay a package of egg noodles. The mother craned her neck come on come on. Girl steadied, observing tabloid banners. Mother slipped a five into the girl's rhinestoned purse, said, "Why don't you pay this time Little Miss Grown Woman?"

6. Gray stripes on the walls at the Hampton Inn Extended Stay seemed appropriate to the father. A wallpapered prison for the middle-aged no worse than the previous wallpapered prison (the mother's pick—expansive blue and black flowers). A whole world of prisons! The father turned animal, twice filled his ice bucket and dumped the contents on the concrete balcony, jumped up and down to hear the crack crack crack. A man got into a car. The father's wife and daughter in the parking lot, and time to be human again.

7. "A sad situation," the babysitter told friends lounging at night on her parents' screened-in porch. She planned years from now to marry the boy holding her hand, though he'd

quit his job and all summer hung around his mother's pool smoking cigarettes with his mother. Dark ahead; behind them bright inside with television and bills, an electric piano and screwed-together models from kits. The babysitter said, "Stay together for the child," and one friend said, "Yes," and another said, "No," and another said, "Life is life," and the boyfriend said nothing.

8. A man with a bare face—no moustache. The twitch of his sharp muscles made the girl nervous, the view of his top lip, the shape of words meant for her mother. Long candles glowed in the center of the table, a bowl of fruit tasted waxy—the girl had tried them earlier after her mother said "You can't." An extra fork had appeared beside the girl's plate. She took one in each hand and learned to eat quickly.

9. A newspaper—"The Home Times." The babysitter helped with the layout, even wrote an article about the disappearance of a gray tabby beneath the porch. The girl's headlines: Magic Money Appears Where Needed, Shakespeare Beats Dickens in Death Match, Snowflakes from June Still Breathing. The girl shoved her mother's copy beneath her bedroom door. "Impossibilities," the girl's mother said over blueberry waffles. "What all good news makes use of."

PART TWO

1. Only one dream remembered: driving, dead bodies, the word PAPER large and black on a billboard. Sometimes when the mother woke panicked in the gray morning she imagined the dream continued—pulled over and the dead bodies woke up. They staggered toward her car with handfuls of colored fliers, shrieking, "Try this! Try this!" They covered her car with fliers

until she opened her door, and the dead surrounded her, pulled her limbs, called, "Come with me! There's a saying! An expression! A humorous disposition you must try!" This is when the mother pushed off her covers and washed her face vigorously with hot water.

6. The father at the Hampton Inn missed the girl's birthday—called once, twice, opened his mouth—nothing. His hands shoved in the ice-cube-filled sink kept him still. All good dates bring memories. Last year he'd rained confetti on the girl and her mother, and for months they found tiny bright circles between couch cushions and carpet threads and pages of books. Once the mother found one in the collar of her shirt and told the father, "It's a reminder that today's not a party." And the father said, "It was a bad idea. A few seconds of humanity and then too many trips to the trashcan."

2. The girl spent a Saturday morning with a hole puncher and any paper she could find: envelopes, magazines, toilet paper. She confettied the house. When the floors and counters and tables and closets seemed sufficiently lively, she opened her window and littered the berry bush where soggy snowflakes clumped. Like fresh snow. Her hand cramped and burned. When her mother came out of her bedroom, the girl strapped on a party hat and went to see what was the problem.

9. A newspaper—"The Home Times." The babysitter helped with the layout, wrote an article about two teddy bears placed in different rooms to years later find each other again. The girl's headlines: Hampton Inn a Fun Place to Die, Burping Good for Heart, Girl in Need of New Purse: Less Girly. The girl shoved her mother's copy beneath her bedroom door. "Hmm," the girl's mother said over Wheat Flakes. "This paper needs a new publisher."

7. "A sad situation," the babysitter told friends one night a hundred feet above the city. Minutes before, she'd slid open a basement window, jiggled loose the screen, and hopped on her bike, skidded down abandoned streets to the glowing white water tower where her friends waited at the top of a thin ladder with rolling papers—not that she approved, but she wouldn't be left behind. "The girl's lost her role models," said the babysitter, taking a puff but not inhaling, and one friend said, "I've lost mine and my parents are still together," and one said, "I hate my dad," and the boyfriend said, "People who look up to their parents must spend lots of time in cupboards and beneath racecar and princess beds."

5. The mother missed something every night. She tucked her daughter into bed and realized no vegetables. No animal-shaped vitamin. No hug-and-a-kiss. Late, late, late, she snuck into the bedroom and placed a carrot in the girl's purse. Next time—a parrot vitamin. Once she stood in the yellow night-lightened room watching her daughter sleep, the heave of her small chest, and, not knowing what to do, she hugged the girl's purse. She kissed it.

8. A man with a bare face emerged from the mother's bedroom one morning. The girl stopped, hands on hips, and stared behind his shoulder. "Excuse me," the man said, his eyes on the bathroom. "You can't stand there." "I like your pajamas." Finally he turned back to the bedroom, and the girl heard him say, "There's something wrong with your daughter," and the mother said, "Just wait a minute until she's cleared out of the hall."

4. Over summer break, the girl wanted projects similar to school but better. The babysitter assumed a curious mind: the sewing-needled insect dissections, the ketchup-smeared Hamlet diorama—the king and queen as throat-slit teddy bears. "It's not

easy to sew heads back on," the babysitter said, but she played audience to the girl's special gait, her one arm thrown theatrically, and she tried not to notice the bears were the ones she'd reunited after years of circumstantial separation.

3. Screamed in the kitchen one night. The girl's mother and two men the girl didn't much recognize, not even the one her father who neatly tuxedoed smelled of too-strong cologne and ripped a document to pieces over the dinner table. "Now, now," said the bare-faced man. "Now." The girl sent to her room. "That can be recopied," said the mother. Beneath the girl, exhausted breathing. "Divide by me," said the unrecognizable father. "And we both come out dead."

PART THREE

9. "The Home Times"—The babysitter put on assignment to interview the father. *Answered Hampton door in tuxedo. Offered plastic cup of water. Yes—a man. Married, but. Tuxedo wasn't practical purchase so getting practice out of it now. Enjoys new place would I like another ice cube? Choices are difficult young lady. Blows nose. Stares long time at girl. Concludes interview.* The girl's headlines: Search for Paper Thief Continues, Mysterious Living Room Weather, In These Times the Home is a Tired Place. The girl slid the mother's copy beneath her door. "Yes, I read it," the mother said over a cup of weak tea. "He's probably getting that thing filthy."

8. A man with a bare face seen leaving early one morning with an armful of clothes go go go. The girl hole-punched her curtains.

7. "A sad situation," the babysitter told her boyfriend floating in his mother's pool. The boyfriend had his ears beneath the surface

and she wasn't sure he'd heard. Plus she wanted to say it again. So she did. And he said, "Here's a sad situation." He climbed out of the pool and went into his house, and she waited awhile, and then she toweled off and pulled her sun-warmed clothes over her still-wet suit. She went home to her books and lifted each one: A sad situation. A sad situation. The carpet dampened around her.

6. Between wallpaper-prisoned walls, the father bathed in ice cubes, wondered was steady clanking better than furious shaking and upheaval of the foundation. No one's fault his body ran hot. Sufficiently cold, he pulled on his tuxedo and stood on the balcony, watching for other humans.

5. The mother missed something every night. Just home, she wore elastic sweatpants and ruined-neck sweatshirts. The girl watched from the staircase, ready in skirt and Mary Janes, with necklace and sequined purse—"What is it?" the mother asked. The girl stayed silent, while barefoot in the living room the mother walked through bits of paper, toed them high into the air so they fluttered around her. A phone call. An anniversary. The mother missed the father.

4. Over summer break, the girl didn't need a babysitter asking why the confetti. Asking if the girl felt alright, if she wanted to talk, if the babysitter could teach her anything about happy mothers and fathers staying together; perhaps a fieldtrip to the babysitter's house? The girl said, "Last I checked my parents weren't in pieces like a leg here an arm there." The girl confettied. The babysitter watched.

3. Screamed in the kitchen one night, "I'm home!" The father a department-store mannequin run through mud. He looked at the mother. "Let's stop the division." The mother took his hand and they left the kitchen together, two humans, one in sweatpants,

one in filthy tuxedo. Smile, the girl thought, alone and watching them sent to their room. Now. Now, now, now.

2. The girl spent Saturday morning littering the house. Clothes, tax forms, books, photos—shred and chopped and thrown in the air. She filled her small sequined purse. She filled her parents' bed. Yesterday, the babysitter had called the mother, said, "This may be my last day." A celebration.

1. Only one dream. The mother woke next to the father and a pile of paper. She thought up new dreams. She thought up the dead. She thought up new words and faces and natures to try—yes yes she should try! Then she settled the dead down. She settled down beside them.

How to Be a Prisoner

Ben was my summer boyfriend, my "older man," Mom called him. He was twelve, and I was eleven, a skinny eleven, though I believed my breasts appeared acceptable to those who mattered. He lived usually with his mother in Florida. He had a beautiful red face with a scar outlining his jaw from once playing basketball and diving into the pavement. He was known as a diver, though he didn't swim. He even refused to stick his ankles in the baby pool my parents packed with beer and Coke for their parties.

The first Monday of summer, Mom stayed home from work. She had me on trial. Would she have to take a leave or could she trust me alone? No money for a sitter. In our neighborhood, kids ran around like abandoned animals, but we knew to be civilized when we had to.

I made lunch in the microwave, not the stove, which Dad said had the potential to explode when used by small hands. Cheese warmed between two slices of bread. I ate in the living room, reading about different breeds of cats and humming. Multitasking. Mom had the television on in the basement. She already pounded up the stairs once to check on me. She was having fun, pretending to care.

After lunch, Ben turned up outside the picture window carrying some pillowcases. With my hand on the doorframe, I swung toward him and we kissed for the first time in nine months.

"You smell like cheese." He gave me a pillowcase, which was smooth and fancy. "I need to borrow your backyard."

At the top of the staircase, I yelled to my mother, "I'm heading to be responsible out back."

"I'll be watching," she called.

Ben went toward the pine trees, where so many years' worth of needles covered the ground. He dropped to his knees and shoveled piles of them into his pillowcase. He said his dad had a new girlfriend who carried a tape measure in her purse. "At breakfast she measured my height.

"How tall are you?" I asked. Some kids in the neighborhood called him a shorty. Whenever I brought him up they said, "That shorty?" though never to his face.

"The girlfriend asked if I knew you. She called you 'That silly girl who ties something around her chest.' She said that's not what breasts are supposed to look like."

"As if she knows." I sat cross-legged in the needles and sorted out the sharpest. They were increasingly snappy the further down the pile. "Breasts don't all look the same."

"They had a conversation about it." Ben filled another pillowcase. "Dad called your breasts 'hypothetical.' Or, I don't know, 'parenthetical.'"

"Your house is a house of hysterics."

Mom came outside with a watering can. She watered the yellowed weeds near the back porch, watching us. Ben waved and smiled at her, and she took it as an invitation.

"I wondered when someone would have the initiative." She nodded at the stuffed pillowcases. "Garbage bags would hold more."

"Yes ma'am," Ben said. "It so happens I have a need for needles just as you have a need to be rid o' them."

She gave me a look like we were weird. I groaned as she went for the bags. "I'm officially on the chain gang."

"What's wrong with her wrist?" he asked.

"Don't look at my mother."

"It's the color my chin turned a few days after I messed it up." I took a handful of pine needles. "You're a crappy boyfriend."

He took my hand and brushed away the needles. He had a crazy eye that twitched occasionally. "You're a good kid." He kissed me quick on the cheek, watching the backdoor.

With trash bags of pine needles, I followed Ben across the street. The needles pricked through my shirt, but I didn't complain. Up a narrow stairwell and down a short stuffy hall, I wondered which room was his and what it would be like to follow him in and close the door behind us.

Instead, I watched him empty four bags of needles onto his father's sheets. We smoothed the comforter over top so no one could tell what was beneath, and he showed me three small holes in the comforter.

"You notice things better left unnoticed," I said.

We heard the front door open, and my mother, "Mary, you shouldn't be here!"

"Come to the park," I told Ben. "Everyone's there."

"That doesn't excite me." He fluffed one of the pine-needled pillows. The bed was prickly and splotched. "Have fun with your ugly friends."

Instead, I went home with Mom, my wrists crossed behind my back like they'd been handcuffed. "You know how to be nice, young lady," she said. Boys' homes were enemy territory.

I sprawled on the living room carpet until almost dinner. Dad's car pulled into the drive. "There's a gorgeous girl on my floor!" The screen door snapped behind him. He took off his shoes. "How's my doll?"

"Tired and dirty." I turned away from him, toward the kitchen. Mom was making sloppy joes.

"Your mother still mad at me?"

I didn't answer. He tiptoed over me, though there was room to go around.

"Let me see it," I heard him say. I closed my eyes. All afternoon, Ben hadn't kissed me. There was a bed. There was his anger. I imagined how it would feel, climbing into a soft space and getting pricked with a thousand needles. It was almost my turn.

Like Falling Down and Laughing

The students in my first class at Stewart Wade High gathered on metal bleachers. In almost-adult clothes, they held leather bags and waxy-bright books; they were skinny but tall. Stretched little kids. The gym smelled of rubber. In Michigan I'd taught Advanced Junior Lit, but here in Chapel Hill, Brant and I were forced to take what jobs were available. I explained that the kids were responsible for locking up their clothes.

"Someone wants my gym shorts, he can have them," a boy said.

"You'll have to work out in your underwear," I told him.

"You'd make us do that?" a girl asked.

"Just watch your stuff."

Since they hadn't brought exercise clothes the first day, I had my students walk the perimeter of the room in their socks for twenty minutes. They moved sluggishly. I encouraged them to talk to each other. "Walk and talk!" I ran across the gym, clapping a few times for the different groups, creating energy. I shouted optional subjects each time they completed a lap: "Pets!" "Favorite Games!" "Assets of Education!"

The kids wearing sandals had to sit on the bleachers and watch. I tried to ignore them. I tried to ignore how the landscape of my body had changed since college. Cellulite had gathered. Excess hung over the elastic of my gym shorts. Brant and I hadn't had sex since the move: we feigned exhaustion or distraction; we looked away when the other was changing, like we suspected our loss in quality employment had taken a toll on our bodies and we were afraid to see the cost.

One student, Ingrid, had her ears pierced all the way up. She had hoops and sparkly studs and little silver crosses. When she saw me looking, she said, "One for every breakup." She walked beside a girl with a parrot tattoo arched around her shoulder. These bodies were poised for rebellion.

—๛—

Brant had wanted to move to Chapel Hill to be near his mother. She'd occasionally overnighted baked goods to us in Michigan and the postage cost so much we could've bought five loaves of bread or a month's worth of cookies. But when we lost our jobs three months ago, his mother sent a Concern Package every other day. Brant felt bad to the extent I met the mailman in the hall and ripped off the stickers. "Add it up," Brant said. "She should spend that on pillows and those hats with flowers pinned to them. She should live propped on pillows, wearing a series of fancy hats." He insisted we live near his mother for more convenient delivery.

The day we moved into our new apartment, Brant's mother brought us a doormat printed with three rows of ladybugs. Their bodies touched on all sides, except the word WELCOME interrupted the middle row. She wore turquoise jewelry and a cardigan embroidered with baby penguins. Since her husband died, she was crazy about grandbabies. When with us, she followed strollers around museums and insisted we sit near the loudest screaming infants in restaurants.

Her eyes watered when she stepped into our apartment, saw the scuffed floors, the walls with odd smears and holes. Boxes outlined the rooms, shoes trailed from paper bags, and our furniture was gathered in haphazard clumps. In the kitchen, the metal cabinets had corroded: big chunks were missing. We had nowhere to put our cleaning supplies. The garbage sat in the middle of the living room.

Brant didn't look at her. "Welcome to our fake life." He pulled stuffing from boxes. He threw Styrofoam peanuts and newspaper balls gently at me.

It was a parade. Pieces clung to my chest, shoulders, and hair. I smiled because this wasn't really our life. This was a moment we stepped off track with plans to arrange things perfectly before stepping back on.

A silk carnation pinned to his mother's straw hat drooped over the brim. She gripped the welcome mat with both hands in one corner. It kept slipping. It hung angled over her legs.

I bent down and examined the mat. "We're not really in a welcoming state."

"You'll be glad for the color coming home," she whispered, positioning it in the hall.

—⚬—

Until last spring, we'd been saving. Brant and I graduated with education degrees and were career-counseled into jobs teaching English at different high schools. We moved from student housing to a suburban apartment complex manicured with small, round bushes against the buildings, trim green grass, and plots of marigolds and pansies in the medians of the parking lots. We put money away each month. We accumulated an eclectic mix of furniture, one piece at a time. We talked about going off birth control.

But we did not have tenure. At the end of our third year teaching, when we lost our jobs, our luckier colleagues gave us bottles of wine and In Sympathy cards with orchids on the front or delicate birds against a pink-gray dusk. Like we had died. We went home to our grown-up apartment, drank wine, and lay frowning on the couch, our legs tangled together. We had furniture all around us. The walls were white and covered with odd prints and paintings we'd bought on art walks.

"You can't lock in a thing like adulthood," I said.

Brant reached for the bottle of red wine and knocked it over. The wine soaked into the white carpet. He kicked my legs getting up and stumbled toward the kitchen, where I assumed he'd get a towel. Instead he came back with a steak knife and began sawing the couch arm's upholstery. "Our life's over here," he said.

I tried to pull him off. "We can take things with us."

He struggled against me and went on sawing. Threads and thin strips of fabric fluttered to the ground, and I looked around for a way to stop him. I unbuttoned my shirt and threw it at him. He kept sawing, but he glanced at me as I took off my bra and clumsily unzipped my skirt. My head pounded from all the movement. He dropped the knife and helped me with the tights.

—⚬⚬⚬—

My students only liked the kicking part of kickball. They ran full speed at the giant red ball, and they got it in the air. But they jogged slowly toward the bases. They swung meekly at pop-ups, short-armed throws to first base.

"Hustle it up!" I called. Teaching gym felt like taking care of people. I developed a shouting voice. I tried to get them excited about physical fitness.

Ingrid hung around sometimes at the end of class. She told me about her boyfriend, David, who was in my third period. "He thinks you're hot." She helped carry the bases to the supply closet. I had a free period next and didn't trust leaving things out.

"He digs curly hair," she said. "I do too, clearly."

David had dark curly hair. He had a tongue ring and a wry smile, and he played bass. I was flattered these kids liked me. In high school I wore combat boots and limp flowery skirts and thickly lined my eyes. Now I wore no makeup. I wore tennis shoes and cotton shorts and pulled my hair back in a clump.

"He asks about you," I told Ingrid. "He wants to know how you scored, and then he tries to beat you."

Ingrid nodded. "You have to find ways to prove you're better. Or else why bother sleeping together." She dropped the bases in the closet, and I locked the door. I wasn't surprised these kids were having sex. I watched her walk across the gym.

—⟋⟍—

Our ladybug doormat sat in the hall outside our apartment—we were the only tenants who had one. Sometimes Brant and I came home and found the mat in front of a different door. Where did we live? We didn't know if people moved it as a prank or if they were overcome with jealousy. We never asked, just pulled the mat back in front of our place, number 39, and went in quickly and locked the door.

Since Brant couldn't find a job, he was forced to substitute when positions came available. "I'm working with six-year-olds," he said. We ate Indian takeout in the kitchen, ripping naan to pieces. "I introduce them to letters. Meet Mr. *C is for cinnamon and also for carrot*. Mr. *Ch is for choke*. We sound out the words."

He pulled at the stretched neck of his T-shirt. He had short blond hair and a trim goatee. He was capable of looking like someone who knew something. But every day he came home, threw his loafers at the wall, and put on these old torn T-shirts he had worn in college. The sleeves reached his elbows.

"Those kids are still developing," I said. "You're teaching them how to be humans."

Brant picked up a steak knife and carved into our Ethan Allen table. It was a beautiful table. I tried not to look.

"I want to know what they think," he said. "I ask them if they like a sentence, one of those subject-verb-whatevers—*Jane walks away*—and they just stare at me. They don't even know what it means."

"Your mother's crazy about kids," I reminded him.

"She's the real deal," he said. "She's in a place to love everyone." He worked the knife deep into the wood. "You should see what these kids bring to Share Circle. Pearls and Rolexes and stuffed animals so big they're like extra students with their own necklaces and watches."

Brant's carving resembled a heart; he ran the blade over and over the perimeter. I put the leftovers in the fridge and watered the spider plant I'd bought at the grocery.

"I don't approve of that accumulation," Brant told me.

"Your mom's right. We might as well have some color in our non-life."

—◊◊◊—

A couple weeks later, Ingrid came to my office. She had a fierce expression. "I can't stop digging them." She showed me her thumbnails jammed beneath the nails of her middle fingers. The creases filled with blood.

I took her hands and flattened her fingers against my palms. "You only own yourself," I said.

"There's no more room on my ears," she told me. "And I refuse to get a tongue ring. I won't give him that."

When David came to third period, he waved, and I ignored him. It was unprofessional to hold a grudge. He stretched near me on the court. "Hey Ms. Windsor, I guess you heard. It's the crash of the year." He gave me a smile like there was a conspiracy.

"Is there something funny about it?"

"Well, it's life." He watched a pretty girl enter the gym in her street clothes. She had long black hair she never pulled back. She had three friends who followed her around. This was the second day in a row she came to class in jeans, a large V-neck, and necklaces to her navel. She climbed the bleachers without saying anything. Other girls watched.

"Get on the court!" I yelled. I had the basketballs out; kids worked on their jump shots.

The girl put her arms around her stomach and rocked forward. Two girls walked toward the bleachers to see about her, and one of them paused and whispered to me, "She gets wicked cramps."

I sent the girls back to the court and climbed the bleachers myself. I'd seen this before: bodies used as an excuse. I had a male gym teacher in middle school that let pale, anxious-looking girls out of class with no questions asked.

"Exercise helps those kinds of cramps," I told the girl.

"I can't today." She frowned. She rocked forward and let out little moans. She was beautiful in a way that bored and exhausted me.

On the court, the balls stopped bouncing. Several students watched.

"Is she alright?" David asked.

I didn't even look at him.

"Go to the nurse," I told the girl. "If you can't participate, don't bother coming at all."

—❧—

Once more, the welcome mat was gone. Brant and I had gone to a Chinese restaurant with his mother and let her pay for us. I'd given my fortune cookie to Brant, and he'd scowled when he read the slip of paper. He ripped it to pieces and threw it on my plate. "That one's yours," he said.

We searched our hall for the doormat. We went to the first floor; we went to the second. At the end of the second floor, Brant punched one of the small clouded windows overlooking an alley. The glass shattered in long shards that further shattered on the carpet.

I ran toward him, expecting doors flung open, sirens, a night in the jail wait-room. A dozen small cuts covered from his knuckles to near his elbow.

"I loved that mat," he said. "It was so nice of my mom." One-handed, he unbuttoned his shirt. I helped him. It was the first move I'd made toward him in weeks. Lately, at night, Brant always wanted to have a hand on me. On my stomach, locked under my arm, resting on my hip. He read somewhere that skin-on-skin contact increased your happiness, and he was willing to try. To me, it felt like possession. Like if my body belonged to him then he had two bodies, and this made him stronger.

No doors opened. We tied the shirt around Brant's bloody hand and finally found the mat on the fourth floor, in front of the last door of the hall. Brant pounded on the door with his left hand, but nobody answered.

"It's nice to know you can get things back." He made a show stepping on the word WELCOME, and he grinned as though this could become a joke we shared. "Thank you," he told the mat.

Inside our apartment, he took off a loafer and handed it to me. In college, Brant had worn sneakers so ragged you could see his toes, and while we talked once at a party, someone pulled off Brant's sneaker and ran away. "That's an important shoe," he'd told me. By the time we left, his sock was beer-soaked, and he refused to sully the shoe we'd finally found in the oven. I carried the sneaker for him like a purse, dirty laces slung over my shoulder. That was the first night we slept together.

I held his brown loafer in our leaf-cluttered entryway, and dirt crumbled into my hand. Lately he threw his shoes into the middle of the room, and I had to leave them or put them away. The loafer was a sad thing to me. I lined it next to mine by the wall and locked the bathroom door while I showered.

Afterward, I tripped over a winter boot in the hallway. Shoes were scattered around the floors and the furniture; he'd gotten into the seasonal shoes and the event shoes, and there were flip-flops and never-worn Kenneth Coles and the three-inch sage heels I hadn't seen since my aunt's wedding.

In the kitchen I found the floor blood-streaked and littered with bits of leather. Brant's brown loafer lay destroyed on the cutting board. I reorganized as best I could, though shoes were hidden in appliances and beneath couch pillows. I found two in the hall, but still several went missing, so some pairs were no longer paired.

Later, when I climbed into bed, I brushed my foot against Brant's shoe, the one he'd left on. I couldn't tell if he was sleeping or pretending. I reached for his hand, the one not wrapped in bloody gauze and discoloring the sheets. He took my hand and squeezed it.

—⁂—

For several weeks after the breakup, Ingrid came to class glowering. She swung a bat so hard it flew from her hands toward a group of girls, who ducked, shielding their faces. When she failed to break seven minutes for the mile, she punched the side of the bleachers and broke one of her fingers. I told her to go to the nurse, and she stared at me until her friend with the parrot tattoo led her away.

She sometimes stopped by my office in her free period. I had a toaster on my desk; I bought strawberry Pop-Tarts because I knew she loved them. She showed me a tiny X she'd scratched into her forearm with a paperclip.

"That isn't a great form of expression," I told her. "Maybe you could find another distraction."

"It's not a distraction." She had her feet propped on my desk; she wore tight black pants that zipped at the bottoms. Between bites of Pop-Tart she leaned forward with her lighter and flickered flames at the frayed bottoms. Her ankles reddened. "I know what I'm doing."

"How can you know something like that?"

"It's not hard to have a plan. It's the only thing that matters." She dropped her legs and crawled onto the desk toward me. Her lips were red and swollen as though chewed-on. She kissed my jawbone near the ear, and then she kissed me on the lips. It happened so quickly I didn't move until she pulled back and offered me a bite of her Pop-Tart.

The pastry broke as I took a piece of it; red and white crumbs littered my desk. I narrowed my eyes like I knew what she was talking about.

"This is good," I said. "I thought it would be too sweet."

We had a moment when I imagined our expressions looked exactly the same.

—⚡—

One evening, Brant's yuppie friends from high school came over and repositioned the furniture. They yelled and laughed about teenage exploits: smoking Romeo y Julietas in the woods, wearing big-legged jeans, raising hell at the Mothers' Bake-off.

"Welcome," I said and then excused myself to the bedroom, where I shut the door and got under the covers to watch reruns of shows I'd loved in High School: *Roseanne, Home Improvement, Beverly Hills 90210*. I couldn't think about Ingrid. I thought about the rest of them: my students' apathy so thick their eyes stayed constantly out of focus. I couldn't get them excited; they blinked at me several seconds after I gave instructions. And I hated that pretty girl with her times-of-the-months that occurred several times a month. She didn't look so sick after class talking to David.

When Brant's friends left, I heard them congratulating themselves in the hall. Brant came in and turned off the television. He swayed in front of it, looking at me.

"I wish I could go in reverse," he said. "There's this space when you're smart enough and young enough to cook things up."

"My students run so slow," I mumbled, half asleep.

He stumbled around, taking off his khakis. "You want to have sex?"

"I can't this week," I said. "My period's an ice machine."

He climbed into bed, pulled the covers away from me, and bunched them up around him. "Let your students go slow. There's nothing good on the other side."

—॥॥—

I did not often wish for a simpler time. My girl students traded body secrets like currency, whispering of homemade tattoos and arms slashed with safety pins and vomiting and fucking on foosball tables. The pretty girl and her friends lay moaning on locker-room benches. I found them once in their underwear in a shower stall, sniffing markers.

Ingrid's self-destruction diminished; she regained her regal posture and wore sleeves covering her markings; she pierced the thin end of her eyebrow. Every day now she came to my office and closed the door, and she kissed me.

Sometimes she sat on my lap or crawled across my desk or took hold of my hair and pulled me that way from my seat. I was careful not to initiate. I imagined myself a doll, willing to accept inflictions the girl needed to inflict. It was a type of therapy.

After we kissed for a while, Ingrid was nice. She made Pop-Tarts and held my legs in her lap, petting my shins. She told me about David's obsession with her body: how he'd smoothed her hair and traced her birthmarks and sniffed her armpit. "When we started fighting, I didn't let him touch me. Not even the filthy pads of my toes."

"I never saw it like that," I said. "I never saw pushing Brant away as a punishment." When I wanted Brant to pay attention to me, I used to take off my clothes.

—॥॥—

Some nights I came home and found the furniture turned upside down, the undersides hacked at. Some nights I found the kitchen full of white smoke and Brant lying beneath the blaring fire alarm with his eyes closed. Some nights he stabbed a knife into his bedside table, and I listened to the dull thuds, no longer caring about this furniture I once wouldn't allow a glass of water to sit upon. Brant made me nervous, but I understood the destruction. These things he did I did too, only differently.

The night I came home to an empty apartment, I knew Brant was at his mother's. I pretended to sleep when he returned late at night, when he removed his shoes and placed them on my stomach and arm. He talked while he undressed: about the hot-air balloon mobile hanging from his bedroom ceiling, about the cartoon movies his mother kept above the television. I couldn't move. I tried to keep the shoes balanced.

After a few evenings of him gone, I drove to his mother's place and saw his red Oldsmobile half on the curb, the front wheels twisted toward the house. I wanted to go inside, bring Brant home and hand him a knife and tell him it was better. But I was afraid to see whatever sadness he unloaded onto his mother.

When Brant got home that night, he put his shoes on my stomach. "I'm considering living with my mother."

In the silence that followed, I sensed him watching me. I turned onto my side and let the shoes fall to the floor. He shook me a few times after that, but I didn't open my eyes.

—⟡—

Every day before lunch, Ingrid came to my office, and we walked together to the cafeteria. In the high-ceilinged room not so different from the gymnasium, the periphery lunch tables were empty. Everyone squeezed around the few tables in the center; they packed in so many chairs some tables had a double circumference. No one was willing to sit alone.

I'd become friendly with Angela, a fifty-something woman who taught printmaking and had Ingrid and her friend with the parrot tattoo in one of her classes. Ingrid and I found Angela and the friend in the faculty corner. I sat next to Ingrid, brushing her arm.

"You have to make it through high school," Angela told the girl with the parrot tattoo. "Everyone's wrapped up in the culture or rebelling against the culture. It all spins around that."

"You know, there's more culture outside," the girl said. "There's culture all over the place." She and Ingrid shared sushi rolls they'd brought in little Japanese boxes with sticks of bamboo drawn across the tops.

"My boyfriend moved out," I told them, suddenly proud to have had this happen to me. "He calls from his mother's. He says soon, when he's ready, we'll get hitched."

"Sounds like an asshole I'd fall for," said Ingrid's friend. She was quick with the chopsticks from the box to her mouth. She sucked on a piece of ginger.

"He says I'd be a good mother," I said. "Like his."

"Do not marry him," Ingrid said.

"It's common for twenty-somethings to move back with their parents," Angela said. "Fuck society, they think. It's easier to have your parents love you."

Some nights I heard scratching on my door and in the morning found hacked strips of wood covering the mat. It didn't make sense given Brant still had a key. I never chain-locked the door, pretending instead that he would come home any minute.

—⋙—

I told myself it was a phase, more of this non-life business. Something we could laugh about eventually, like with the doormat, like *Mr. Ch is for Choke*. Like losing your balance is funny. You sit on the floor for a while, and then you get up.

I went to Brant's mother's. I had this idea I could laugh at Brant now, and he would laugh too, and the ridiculousness could be over.

His mother answered the door with a floury ball of dough in her hands. "He's in a fragile state," she said. Her muscles bulged as she worked her fingers through the dough. Watching her made me almost want to move in, too. She had a carefully put-together house, with floral trim lining the walls and a big cherry cabinet to hide coats and shoes. The carpet had fresh vacuum lines; a sprinkler sputtered arcs around the backyard.

I found Brant lying in bed. On the floor around him, he'd built up a Lego town: blue, red, and yellow houses with their angled roofs in steps. But G.I. Joe dolls were stationed outside each door, like they were taking over. Little Lego people posed mid-walk. They had broad-smiling, idiot faces.

"I'm still working," he told me. "Eventually we'll have enough money to buy a house and have kids, and then we'll have the real deal. We'll move right over."

"I thought you hated kids. And their poor understanding of sentence structure."

He blinked at me. He focused on my mouth, like he couldn't understand it. "This is a lovely place. Here we're supposed to love each other."

"This isn't our place," I said.

"This is how you get me." He lifted his hands above his stomach and made an explosion noise.

I drove from his mother's to the grocery and bought three spider plants. At home, I pulled the welcome mat inside the apartment and laid it on the floor, like the apartment was the outside and the world was a place to feel comfortable in. Plants and furniture surrounded me. With a steak knife I hacked away at the couch. I tried to laugh. I laughed.

—⚏—

Again, the pretty girl came to third period in her street clothes and sat on the bleachers with her arms around her waist.

"Get on the court!" I yelled. My students were stretching. I would line them up for relays today; I had five blue batons. I was trying for camaraderie.

"I can't!" the girl said, sobbing.

I took her into my office. The nurse had given me some ibuprofen for times-of-the-month. I handed her the bottle. "Your classroom decorum grade includes originality," I told her. "I pulled this crap in *my* gym class."

After a few minutes, the girl walked onto the floor in her gym clothes, her face tear-streaked. She'd pulled back her hair. She slumped toward the rest of us.

When the race began, the kids cheered, and with those around them cheering, everyone tried to out-scream the others. The pretty girl ran anchor in her group, and she ran her heart out. I saw the pain on her face. When she finished in second place, she threw the baton on the ground and leaned against the wall. David jogged over and put his hand on her back.

She moaned.

Another girl put her head between her knees and said she felt sick. Then another and another, until I had five girls moaning that they were going to vomit all over the floor. And I started feeling nauseated too, watching them writhe around. I wanted to hold my legs to my chest and whine like I was going to die.

Instead, I sent them to the nurse. Once they were gone, I lined up those who remained, and we had another race. This time I watched from the bleachers. They cheered themselves on.

—⚬—

A week later, in the cafeteria, I spotted Brant at the popular boys' table. He was still substituting, but he didn't sit with the substitutes. He didn't sit with David at the Goth table, or with the hipsters, druggies, or thugs. With his combed hair, his Ralph Lauren sports jacket, he managed to look like he belonged with that cable-knit group of boat-owners, a group that would make his mother proud.

He slouched hungrily forward. The other boys leaned toward him, and Brant's deep laugh spread across the room.

I touched Ingrid's wrist. "That used to be my boyfriend."

Beneath our table, Ingrid had her hand on my leg. Together, with two paperclips, we'd carved a heart on my thigh. Every day now I shaved and slathered my legs with lotion, and it burned.

"Not bad," Ingrid said. "He reminds me of someone I used to be in love with."

I experienced a tiny movement of pride. It was another life. He used to hold my hand and feel happy.

I Now Pronounce You

In bed, the wife heard the sports announcer. Heard the cheers and chants while washing her face in the bathroom—she didn't care. She didn't care her new husband woke before her, the sneak, and went downstairs to watch early-morning sports television. A good decision to marry him—rushed, frantic even, but the wife was two years post-college and sick-of-it, and the husband was an American flag: starry-eyed and pin-striped, a regal flourisher to those beneath him.

Drunk at the Hooters bar, the husband had watched her. He'd spoken loudly about the feminist movement and embracing one's sexuality. "Nobody has to hide beneath the covers anymore," he'd said, and she'd believed him.

Good to be a wife. Just back from her honeymoon, in the center of the clean-carpeted, big-roomed house—it was his—she adjusted. She had previously rented a gritty-floored apartment above a beauty salon that emitted all sorts of smells and chemicals; she believed she'd become more beautiful walking constantly through them. Sometimes she locked herself in the new husband's bathroom and hair-sprayed the walls and foamed mousse into the sink. On the toilet, she closed her eyes and remembered fretful, feral nights silky-legged with Hooters friends, and when she emerged steamed in the doorway, riotous and beautiful, she and the new husband gambled. Striptease Poker. Seven-Card Pose. Texas Hold-This.

Mornings, if she made enough noise on the stairs, the new husband turned off the television. He smiled from the couch and she, the new wife, said, "I heard something," and the new husband said, "I didn't mean to wake you!"

Good to be a newly-wed. She didn't care about the television. Her father too had been a sports fanatic, kept a game on all meal-times, which he spoke to directly while the rest of them communicated with brief addresses and subtle eye movements.

The new husband was content to be a husband. While she cooked, he swiveled on a kitchen stool explaining his spoon and spatula ordering, the gadgets string-strung above the stove. Cooking used to be a hobby belonging to him, but he wished the new wife to feel useful given she'd quit her job, given he was a successful flag and couldn't be married to a Hooter no matter how much she shocked the system.

He ate his scrambled eggs and toast separate. He refused to eat anything burnt even if she cut off the black parts—he could tell and it wasn't the same.

"Take it up with the kitchen," the new wife told the new husband. They sat in the dining room, which was large and previously empty; the husband had kept many rooms this way, like open terminals scattered through the house, waiting, perhaps, for a pre-packaged family to move in and stuff them with baggage. From her apartment, the new wife had contributed various items that weren't too torn or beer-stained, such as her folding card table: they sat here now. A pile of red and black chips lay in the middle.

"I like this place very much," said the husband. He brushed some egg from the corner of her mouth. "I'll come here all the time. But the food sucks."

"Nobody comes for the food," said the new wife. "This is the twenty-first century." She pawed his beard as though he had egg on his face too.

"Food is a necessity," he said. "Kids, television, church, counseling—all the Great American Pastimes. After marriage, there is a husband and a wife."

The new wife had on her plate four slightly burnt pieces of toast. The new husband had the sports page. Chewing her toast, she appreciated his handsomeness. To honor, to cherish. She appreciated the cheers from those side-lined enthusiasts, from her old Hooters friends, from the announcer. And with the true smell of hot dogs and the stickiness of beer born-and-brewed, the American flag waved above the field, and it was saluted.

Good to be a newly-wed. The husband and the wife: they were to be successful together. 'Til death. 'Til death. The wife was encouraged to believe it. So she believed it.

—⁓—

But sooner or later, in good times and in bad. In sickness and in health.

In the husband and wife's third year of marriage, a woman— not the wife—pushed the no-longer-new husband from a third-story window after she'd slightly burnt some chicken and he'd refused to eat it. And also he had refused to leave his no-longer-new wife for the other woman because he'd realized the other woman was crazy. Besides, it was nice with the wife, who didn't complain when he watched sports in the morning and who stayed home and became a better cook and took care of their small son, whom he didn't much like but planned to increasingly as the son came to resemble more a small man than a wild animal.

All these feelings and missteps blurted to the no-longer-new wife in the emergency room overwhelmed her. Also, her no-longer-new husband would be ugly forever and have a limp and so could never move speedily from the house to the car when they were late for something—church, yoga, marriage counseling, Buddhist meditation—and they were always late due to his sports-watching and his loud, lengthy disagreements with the television and the newspaper early in the morning.

Good to be a wife! Good to have the decision made pretty much for her: Stand by. Stand by. She nodded at the foot of the bed. She fell sideways into the nurse. The baby cried and the wife laid him gently on the floor. "I think he's hungry," she told the nurse. The wife ran from the room.

"You are a steel pole," her mother said when the wife called from a bathroom stall in the hospital lobby. The wife opened her purse and lined her makeup along the rim of the toilet. Her mother said, "Your husband's a flag just caught up in the wrong kind of wind."

"Can you be more specific?" the wife asked. She sniffed her powder puff. She hairsprayed the stall around her.

"You let that man tie himself to you and now everyone's seen him waving."

"But this is the twenty-first century!" The wife applied lipstick. Eyeliner—thick; blush—like her face would explode. "I'm allowed to be flagless."

"This is a test. If you take the flag down now that it's crippled, you're a failure as a wife, as a woman, and as a human being."

Good to be a wife. How easy and admirable to stay with her husband, which is what she did, and she took care of him. On the day he came home, she helped him up the stairs. He hadn't looked at her directly since his first day at the hospital, and even now, a month later, he sighed frequently on the steps and turned away when she caught him staring.

"Let's move on with it," she said.

"You're a model." He couldn't quite lift his legs enough to clear each step. He tripped without her close attention. Skin doctors had patched his face decently, though of course he would be scarred for life. He started crying. "You are a good wife!" It was painful for him.

"I'm a steel pole," she said.

Every day the husband remained in bed until the wife was willing to help. She brought him to the dining room, where they ate all meals together: the wife, the husband, the baby in highchair, at an expensive wood table purchased from a fancy furniture store. The table was narrow and long, the kind where you could sit very close to each other or very far away. Still a pile of gambling chips lay in the middle. Still the husband and wife gambled a few nights each week after the son went to bed, only instead of clothes and positions, the wife tossed in words with her chips: "Dignity," "Independence," "Life Free of Straitjackets."

The husband cleared his throat, and when he won he said, "Although I now own your Hopes and Dreams fair-and-square, I'd like you to keep them."

"Take them," she said. "They're rocks tied around my swollen ankles."

Little sports were watched. Since for a long time the husband couldn't move by himself, he had to ask from the bed, "Dear, would you mind? The television for a while?"

"The television is very contemporary," the wife said. "Also, that girl you fucked. Something contemporary about her."

The husband batted the sheets. He leaned from his propped pillow. "I must act out my masculinity vicariously."

She pushed him back against the pillow. He complied, though his face readied for a tantrum. "Once you get better," she said, "you can act out your masculinity as a traditional man by returning to work and foundationing your family."

However, she lived with a sneak. The moment he could lower himself from bed, the husband woke early and dragged himself downstairs in his boxer shorts. And she heard it. She didn't care! Her husband was alive and watching football. She would treat his knees for rug burns from his vigorous trip across the carpet; at the same time she would cook breakfast and nurse the baby in a cradle-hold across her chest.

Good to be a wife! Good to know she would swaddle down transgression or meanness or need for welfare for the good of the family and the perpetuation of a society in which people stayed together for the good of the family. She had her marriage counseling. She had her prayer and meditation and stretches.

Who cared if she told old Hooters friends she saw on the street, "Don't look at me." Who cared if some mornings, while her husband flexed his masculinity, she pulled out her old Hooters shirt and ripped tights and danced in front of the mirror or in front of the baby, who smiled and laughed in a way very different from her old patrons. The not-so-new wife appreciated her diluted beauty, her diluted sexuality. Occasionally during these early-morning dance sessions, with the applause and announcer beneath her feet, she wondered what would happen when she had a nervous breakdown, perhaps in the grocery store—it seemed a likely place, with all the juicy, squeezable fruit.

—◊◊◊—

The minister had said it, six years ago—she remembered. "I now pronounce you man and wife."

She didn't care about the pronouncement—man, wife. Man. Wife. They'd had a miniature wedding in her parents' backyard with only some blankets to sit on, and everyone who attended was either dead or delirious or so far in her past they were rendered obscure. Now, when the wife saw old friends on the street, she covered her face and ran the other way. A few chased after her, and when they caught her by the arms and saw who she was, they said, "I'm sorry, Miss. I thought you were someone else."

So the husband was a flag, and she a mere wife—one couldn't spend a lifetime worried about being contemporary.

Her first attack hit in the bathroom one morning. She came to the end of her mascara and hurled the pink wand into the toilet. She flushed and flushed, screaming "Why won't you take it?" when the wand resurfaced. Two hours later she came out of the bathroom, soaked in perfume, and when the husband asked what the problem was, she responded in a high voice: "Lady troubles!"

Her second attack hit a week later when she found a pair of pink laced underwear in the husband's tennis shoe. She shredded it to pieces with her fingernails and baked a fun-fetti cake, which she served to the husband. She threw the leftovers in a heap on the back porch and told the dog about it.

Her third attack hit the following day when picking her son up from pre-little-league football. Still in his padding, he hurled himself into the side of the car—this was for fun—and she drove away without him and ditched the car by the side of the highway. An hour later the authorities found her sprawled on the edge of a creek, scooping gray water over her face.

The cop who saves her is a flag, and he feels sorry for her. She reminds him of his mother. His wife. His little girl. In different ways, she is all of them and also every woman he's ever met. She tells the flag on the way to the station. She tells him everything. Her whole life and the history of a society that brought them here. She lives in a house of sports. She suspects the hideous freak flag attached to her pole has found another pole. Most nights she sits at a diamond-studded table gambling away her pride, her body, her life.

The wife wants to know why she has to be the wife. Couldn't she be the flag and the flag be the wife because this is fiction where anything's possible and stories might as well be used for good instead of reinforcing stereotypes.

The cop and the author want to know how a Hooters waitress married to a traditional sports-loving American flag knows and cares so much about the problems with gender roles and how they're perpetuated.

And yes, you have to be the wife because you are the wife. You agreed to these terms when you were married. Furthermore, you are a woman. You agreed to these terms when you were born, debatably, but certainly when you bought your first dress, when you painted your room pink, when you worked the job you worked through college, where you mastered so many seductive salutes you were voted Little Miss Patriot. And now you're on your way to a nervous breakdown, which is traditionally a female condition, and you are headed to jail and then probably to a mental institution, where you will be kept for your flags to visit at their leisure. They will bring you flowers and chocolate and you will be glad to have them. Even if this story took place in some alternate reality on some undiscovered planet where all titles were flags and shoe sizes were equal and everyone opened doors for each other and walked naked without judgment; even if flags allowed sorry specimens to flap among them, you, the wife, could never pull off stars-and-stripes.

Buttons

Before the trip to Grandma's, I emptied my closet and cut the buttons from my clothes. I stuffed them in my pockets and ran my hands through the cold plastic discs the whole way to Lansing.

Mom said, "Be nice." She had bologna and Miracle Whip and a tiny tin of caviar in the cooler between us. She had Wonder Bread and china cups in a plastic grocery bag. "I don't want any observations from you. She doesn't need to hear it."

Grandma's house smelled like lemon cleaner and wet Band-Aids. She had jars of buttons around her living room: a jar of blue, a jar of green, a jar of red. On her coffee table with the clawed feet: a half jar of pink. On her stained-black fireplace: a quarter jar of gray. Tubes trailed from Grandma's nose and disappeared behind a cushion. She wore a smooth yellow smock. Her couch was red and black flowers. When Mom spoke, Grandma looked at the jar on the coffee table.

"With Joel's promotion they gave him a window. So there's the real world while he works and he's a little closer." Mom pulled at some threads on her armchair. She had three rings with diamonds on her fingers. She looked at me, sitting on the floor by the coffee table with my coat still on. "And Celia's become a brat. She takes socks from our dresser and makes sock balls with more than two socks, stretching as many as she can until they're all misshapen."

"The socks like to be close together," I said.

Grandma didn't turn from her buttons. I stared at my zipper and pulled it open and closed. Mom sighed like that's what she meant.

When Mom went to the kitchen, Grandma smiled at me. "Do you like my buttons?" Her voice scratched at first, then smoothed out. Her tubes moved as she spoke.

"Here, I like them." I emptied my pockets onto the coffee table, the buttons spilling, rolling, and crashing into each other.

Grandma held out her hand. "Give me your best."

I moved two pearl buttons into her palm. They came from my most expensive new sweater. "Mom says I'm no good with buttons. Every time, I'm lopsided."

Grandma brought the buttons close to her eyes and didn't speak. Every few seconds, a shake went through her hand and she had to refocus her gaze where the buttons ended up. When Mom creaked in the hallway, Grandma put the buttons in her mouth.

Mom lowered a plate of sandwiches beside my buttons. "More buttons." She took a bite of her sandwich, full of bologna and what looked like little black beads. "I should've brought you a spool of thread." She handed a sandwich to Grandma, who placed it in her lap.

"Eat," Mom told us.

Grandma didn't take a bite, but made a chewing motion with her mouth. I took a sandwich and put it on the floor and chewed air along with her.

Mom stared at the pile of buttons. I thought about sliding some into my mouth. I imagined the cool plastic, my tongue turning the buttons over and over, pressing against the tiny holes just big enough for my tongue to recognize. I thought about swallowing them, how they'd lie in my stomach like they lie in the jars, all different sizes jumbled and pressed together.

January on the Ground

I was having trouble, lately, flitting around. The thing was, people told me about the choices I'd have in college, how I'd learn all this amazing stuff. But there were no classes about bat-eating cults or the origin of jack-o-lanterns or how to carve things in the wood of dead trees. There was a lot of construction—those dusty orange cones—and worksheets covering the same things I'd learned in high school: composing a thesis, the convolutedness of World War One, rules about imaginary numbers. And when I left the dorms and drove across Chapel Hill for another "reasonable" Sunday Family Dinner, it seemed my heart beat normally again. My breathing slowed, my head cleared: just seeing the sturdy brown colonial, the white pillars, the wrap-around porch.

But the inside of my parents' house deteriorated. The rooms had the hastily cleaned feel of a nine-year-old's bedroom: pictures and trinkets awkwardly angled, magazines shoved beneath couches, shoes in a massive pile by the door. Dad sat on the edge of a chair, an afghan folded unevenly beside him, reading his latest *Men's Health*. He had a slightly ashamed, slightly indignant look when I caught him reading it. And Mom developed a fondness for leaving things burning on the stove. She went to the back porch and stood stiffly, her arms bent, her shoulders back too far. She stared into the long flimsy grass and weeds, the weary pine trees. It was unsettling to see, especially once, when rain suddenly poured from the sky, and she stood there, pelted with water—these millions of drops whizzing through the air, flying into her—like someone attacked. Her clothes sagged from the weight. Her pants in the back got so sad and droopy, I had to look away.

I stopped coming to family dinners for a while. But in the middle of finals week, my roommate found me on the floor of our dorm room, wrapped in a soaking wet sheet, face down in a pool of chunky tequila-spiked vomit. I don't really remember what happened. I'd watched a special on mummies that week and thought it had something to do with that: like I wanted to pre-serve myself, like I wanted my body to survive even if I didn't.

My parents thought I was depressed or hated myself; they refused to see the ego involved in the mummification attempt. But I agreed to come home and be "reasonable" for a while. Whatever that meant.

—ෆ—

My parents always made a big deal about New Year's. The crash-ing of Eve into Day, that twirling ball, the screaming people on the streets, and us in the living room with the lights off, watch-ing, whispering, waiting for that release, the heavy baggage of the past year lifted with three words, the first, of course, being "Happy." We jumped off the couch. We loved America. We loved each other. We looked forward to the dozen clusters of fresh days ahead of us. We smiled in our sleep that night. We tried to carry the feeling into January as long as possible.

This year, I woke New Year's Day to Jack paying excruciating attention to my hair. Raking his hands through it. Yanking out an occasional strand. Officially Carrie and I had spent the night with some sweater-wearing, straight-haired girls in the suburbs. My par-ents hadn't cared about the particulars. I'd missed the countdown, the leap, the kisses; and for this betrayal Mom had placed a fringed couch cushion in front of her face and waved me away.

"Ouch." I only half-cared if Jack stopped. I was trying not to care about things anymore, and that's usually how far I got. Half.

"There's glitter in it," Jack said and continued raking. He would come to my mother's luncheon that afternoon. I'd blurted the offer last night after refusing to have sex, lying beside him with our bare legs touching. Carrie would drive home for the rest of Winter Break today, and I needed someone there distracting me from relatives whispering about my Emergency Room visit and my dropping out of college.

Elsewhere in Jack's apartment, people were moving around. Someone laughed, there was some thumping, and the front door slammed. I threw back the sheet and got out of bed. Somewhere among the stacks of dusty graphic novels and bongs, collapsed plywood shelves, and balls of socks scattered around the toe-curlingly gritty carpet, I would find my jeans.

"You've got skinny legs," Jack said.

"You've got a fat head," I told him; although he was gorgeous in a roll-in-the-mud, set-his-hair-on-fire sort of way. He was the kind of person who showed up randomly on the same sidewalk I happened to be on, with bright scratches on his cheeks or blue candle wax dried into a lock of his hair. He was the kind of person who looked better when met by accident.

There was a knock at the door and Carrie's muffled voice. "Sara. Your phone's been dancing across the table since nine."

"Where's my jeans?" I asked Jack.

He got out of bed and gracefully crossed the cluttered room in his boxers. He opened the middle dresser drawer and pulled out a small folded pair of jeans.

"How'd they get there?"

He waved his free hand in the air and made ghostly noises, "Ooooooo. I put them there."

"All folded like that?"

He grinned as I struggled to pull them on.

"We tried to kill it," Carrie said, handing me the phone in Jack's doorway. "It's got a surprisingly hard shell." She swiped at the damp bangs falling across her forehead.

Jack turned sideways in the doorway to get by us.

"There's something," Carrie whispered. "Last night about three o'clock, a girl came to the door calling for Jack."

"Was she cute?" I asked. "No, forget it." It didn't matter. Jack radiated something everyone wanted, and he gave what he had, passed love out like bread: the fluffy, airy kind.

Jack stood in the space between the living room and kitchenette with his hands on his bony hips, his elbows out, exposing tufts of dark hair beneath his arms. His eyes narrowed in the direction of the television.

"I can't look at a television," I said, grabbing my boots. "I can't even hear it in the morning."

"You want me to clap?" Jack asked. He followed me to the door.

"Twice, right?" I asked, pulling my black leather jacket from a heavy pile of coats. "Like magic."

"I'll block it out." He clapped wildly.

I stumbled through the door, stumbled down the damp, brown-carpeted hall, trying to pull everything on. I'd lost Carrie in the apartment. Jack stood in the doorway.

"I'll see you at three!" he called like I was a thousand feet away instead of ten. "I'll wear a tie!"

I pushed my way into the cold stairwell, where I played with my coat zipper and waited for Carrie. She and I had lived on the same dorm floor; we became fast friends because we were both willing to push things to a certain point: with alcohol, with drugs, with boys. We believed in partial restraint. We believed in backing out at the last minute.

"Hey, crazy," she said, coming through the door in her jacket with the fur around the neck. "He slept with *you*, remember?"

"We didn't sleep together. I'm trying not to have too great a time."

"Pretend he's just some guy."

"He's meeting my parents."

Carrie squeezed my wrist as we went down the stairs. "He likes that sort of thing. He *likes* people."

Outside, a light dusting of snow covered the tops of cars and the swoops of awnings. Everything else was gray, damp, and muddy: this was the worst part about Chapel Hill winters. Only unreachable spots got decorated, those special elevated places. I got tired of walking around on the ground.

"You've got glitter in your hair," Carrie said as we climbed into her cold car. She would drop me at home and I would be alone.

I turned on the heat and leaned over her lap. "Get it out, will you?" I shook my head in her face. "Just rip it all out."

—⚋—

On the way home, it started raining: the slow kind of rain, lethargic and continuous, like droopy silver streamers slinking off the tree. It was just past 10:00 in the morning, and four missed calls from my mother. I'd grown up an "only child," which of course seemed fitting: my whole life I'd been told, "only do it *this way*," "only *stop crying*," "only *do better next time*." My parents liked a routine. When I refused to get up at the standard "reasonable" hour (7:00) on Saturday mornings, my parents crowded into my room with concerned looks and cups of coffee and said, "What's wrong? It's time to get up isn't it? I think it's time to get up."

When I finally answered my phone, Mom said, "People are coming. I need your help."

"I'll be home in fifteen and then I'll be helpful. I've got so much energy right now." I hung up and slumped low in the car seat, feeling exhausted, really, and dried out: my eyes hurt, they felt dangerously stretched.

"Everyone just said 'Yaaay' when the ball dropped last night," I told Carrie. "Nobody said 'Happy New Year.'"

"People don't believe in that anymore," Carrie said.

I watched the rain curl down the window. "I miss the dorms."

"You hated them," Carrie said. "The sinks with the separate H and C faucets. Your roommate's sex calls to Missouri."

"It was expected," I said. "My home's an altered universe. My parents are strange sad versions of themselves."

"They're transitioning," Carrie said. "You've walked in on them in the middle of it." I didn't know anything besides what Carrie told me. She'd stayed at my house the last ten days, and sometimes I found her and Mom whispering—in the hallway, in the stairwell, in the corner by the coffeepot.

Mom told Carrie that when I moved out, the house felt hollow.

Mom told Carrie she feels like she's changing into something she doesn't know what. Something flimsy and up in the air. An antenna. A radio tower. I didn't appreciate being left out, though I was afraid Mom would tell me she was a dangling branch and expect a response like, "Everything will be alright you'll see."

She told Carrie she had no one to talk to who understood anything.

—〰—

When Carrie dropped me off, I stood on the porch watching her car: the squeaky wipers and her face pale and blurry behind them. Mom's voice rose faintly behind the front door: "Let's get rid of these magazines."

Carrie lowered the window. "Hey dreamy, I've got things to do."

"My aunt makes fabulous Mud Pie!"

Carrie's car grumbled into reverse, but she sat there waiting. It was terrifying how this could happen. I'd known her four months and couldn't stand to have her leave.

Finally I waved and went inside. The entryway was cool and well-lit; the house had that pre-party feel when everything seemed expanded, the rooms cavernous and waiting to be filled. A heavy, buttery smell hung in the air, and the house was quiet for a moment after the clicking of the door.

Mom called from the living room. I found her on her knees, shoveling a stack of wrinkled *Men's Health* magazines into a garbage bag. "Quick," she said, and I helped her scoop them in.

"Is that Sara?" Dad called from the kitchen.

"Just your make-believe son!" she called, then said, "Probably if we had a son he'd like this crap, too."

She lifted the heavy garbage bag and headed toward the door, looking beautiful in a long gray wool skirt and a yellow blouse tucked at the waist. Moving from the dorms had been quick with Mom leading the way, throwing candles and coats in boxes, loading her arms with all my hangered clothes and bags of shoes and rolled-up martial-art hero posters. With my stuff piled in the back of the car, my parents had taken me to dinner and suggested over burgers with wavy pickles and fancy ketchup that maybe I wasn't quite ready for college. Maybe I shouldn't have rushed out of the house.

Banging came from the kitchen, and I found Dad bent over the oven. The room was clean for the party other than some faded Rainbow Brite stickers cluttering appliance bottoms.

"See if this is done," Dad said. He had on his dress slacks and a collared shirt unbuttoned at the neck. He hadn't shaved in days. "You smell like smoke," he said as I went to the cupboard for toothpicks.

"I like the smell of cigarettes," I told him. "I don't smoke them, I just hold them. I wave them around my clothes."

"You don't smell like cigarettes," he said. We got the pan out of the oven: some goopy yellow thing. "I decided I wasn't going to eat mud this year."

The front door slammed. Mom came into the kitchen dripping water, her skirt dragging on the ground, her shirt tight and twisted around her arms. "It's *gorgeous* outside," she told us.

Dad sighed.

"It's New Year's," she said warningly. Her makeup had smeared.

"Just get them off," he said. "We'll put them in the dryer."

Mom went down to the basement.

"She's allowed to have fun," Dad told me. He wouldn't say it to her. He hardly said anything to her if he didn't have to.

We stood by the stove, staring at his creation, listening to the hollow noises in the basement: the crank of a dial, the rumblings of hot air pushing things around.

"I invited someone today," I said.

"That's good, Sara," he said. "You're allowed to have friends. Your mother's allowed to have fun. No one's stopping anyone."

I took a dozen toothpicks out of the box and we sunk them into the dessert. We made a smiley face.

Mom came upstairs wearing one of Dad's marathon T-shirts, and she squeezed between us at the stove. She stared awhile at the toothpicks. "How was your girl party?" she asked.

"Awkward," I told her.

She nodded. "Everything's awkward, isn't it? Things get so awkward. That's why eventually people just want to be around family." She linked her arms through mine and Dad's. "Let's plan something for next year. We'll go somewhere. We'll skip the big party."

Dad raised his eyebrows at me. The party had always been my mother's. My mother's family, my mother's food, my mother directing everything from the nucleus, maintaining quality and integrity, while we dashed around carrying out orders.

Still, there was a time we'd all loved parties. When we didn't disappear into bedrooms with people earlier than advisable to escape crowded bongs and kegs and awkward inquiries from those who'd heard about my mummification effort, who might ask in front of Jack: "Are you the one . . . ?"

"Let's skip the party," I agreed.

"Alright." Mom clapped her hands twice. "Now. We've got a lot of shit to do." She took the toothpicks out of the pan.

—⟋⟍⟋—

Guests arrived around 2:55 and lined the kitchen counters with ceramic dishes wrapped in shiny plastic. Everyone asked if we saw the ball drop last night, and Mom described the countdown as if I'd been home, the way it happened last year: with bowls of candy corn and cashews; with the couch, the jumps, the "Happy New Years!"

My aunts looked at me; they smiled, opened their mouths, then went back to smiling. I sat on the couch with my ten-year-old cousin who had pink pom-poms hanging from her ponytail.

"Do you have a boyfriend?" she asked. She kicked her leg against the couch like she was trying to silence it.

"No," I said.

She nodded. "I don't care about a boyfriend. I just want my own house." She kicked thoughtfully. "I don't even care if it gets dirty."

My mother disappeared. Dad sat opposite me with my grumpy uncles, all of them staring at a football recap on television, and I was mad they were getting out of this in some way. The clock read 3:35. I half-expected Jack to fly into the room and make some crazy announcement about flights being cancelled or purses being stolen. But Jack was a certain kind of person. He made you believe you couldn't rely on him. He made you believe you didn't *want* to rely on him. He'd been employed by the strange-smelling co-op near the bank where I worked some days after class. He was a fantastic Frisbee player; he had this graceful way of jumping for the disc and twisting his body around mid-jump in a sort of half-bow. He played sometimes outside the co-op, and people stopped to watch. People clapped.

Of course I had never played Frisbee, but whenever I felt depressed about school, or whatever, I went into the co-op and half-followed, half-ignored him. I had developed this demeanor like I was too good for everyone. I allowed myself to get very pale. I wore a lot of black with belts.

One day Jack put down the organic soups he was stocking and walked with me to the register. "Are you one of those bank people?" he asked.

"Not one of *those* bank people," I told him. It was a point of embarrassment. My dad knew the regional manager.

"It seems like a lot of mirrors around the outside," Jack said. He took the pasta salad and soda from my hands and put them on the conveyor belt. "Those mirrors would make me nervous." He unbuttoned the cuff of my shirt and sort of fanned it out around my wrist.

I watched him do this. "They're windows," I said. "From the inside."

I heard he got fired from the co-op. I didn't see him for weeks; and then one day I ran into him on my way to Freshman Comp.

"What do you know," he said, and he stopped in the middle of the busy campus path so everyone walked around him. Leafy shadows played across his face, and I noticed the thick greens above us and the feathery clouds beyond them.

"The sky's a nice texture today," I said.

He agreed, and we went back to my dorm room and made out a little. I didn't even mind the sweat stains beneath his arms, his giant jeans, the mud on his shoes. I kept picturing him flying through the air after that Frisbee, and it was beautiful.

Finally I got off the couch. Dad said, "There's Sara!" He toasted me with his glass.

"Here's me," I said, as I had as a child, though of course it came out differently.

In the kitchen my two aunts at the dessert table quit talking. I didn't look at them. Where was Mom? I took a piece of my Dad's gooey butter cake, the first one.

"Looks like Sara's got a good piece of cake," my aunt said.

I took a bite and wondered how I looked to them. I didn't feel fragile or dangerous or however out-of-control women appear to those with white knuckles gripping a steering wheel, peering around, going slow.

"It's really good cake," I said. But I didn't want it anymore. I put my paper plate in the sink.

I got my jacket from the hall and went onto the porch, the warm air parting like a curtain. And I found them there on the grass, standing close in the drizzle: Mom and Jack, my mom crying these extended moan-hiccups, and Jack nodding and motioning with his hands. He had on a beige sports jacket that was torn and ragged at the bottom. I couldn't see if he wore a tie. I imagined he wasn't.

I sat on the steps as Mom leaned into Jack. He put his arms around her. The whole thing was embarrassing. My mother in the arms of a guy who loved everyone.

Dark leaves collected on the ground by the stairs; cracks ruptured the wet walkway from my feet to the driveway. The world had a sweet smell, something fresh, something that could've been cleansing. I didn't look at my mother. I leaned against the wall and only half-cared if they noticed.

Ruckus, Exhaustion

In a van with two bench seats, the boys slept. Taped blankets over windows blocked fussed-up brush and green road announcements, and when the parents pointed roadside they pointed out only to each other. A lump of squirrel. A farmhouse painted pink. An elephant cloud split open just ahead, just above, immersion. Cross into Virginia and the up and down of green mountains, fruit pies and cow pies, stretches of puffed trees ready for picking. To the father, Virginia meant driving through a blast-radius of history. The mother kept her excitement at a low-boil.

A diner in Winchester—here they stopped for burgers and slow-cooked pudding; the boys emerged blinking in jackets too warm for this damp heat with the collars high and sleeves shoved to the elbow. How they must look beside their high-waisted short-panted parents. Wet outside, but a protected table and a rain-slickered girl in rollerblades.

"History happened here," said the father.

"Also, there," said the mother. "And there."

"Don't point at me," said the youngest; "Nor me," said the oldest; and they slunk into their coats and stared at rim-crusted bottles of ketchup and mustard.

"No pressure," the father said. "History will be written with or without you."

Inside the restaurant: antlers, signed photos, glassed-in flags, but people saw only their food or each other or dimly the floor. The mother watched through the rain-dotted window. Collections on walls: a poor man's riches.

Twenty hours from home to finish, the drive 95 percent of the battle. The youngest, thirteen, collected for shop-lifting and now grounded to a van and all the trappings Motel 6 pull-up-to-your-room-and-vomits had to offer. He unwrapped soaps. Trips to vending machines allowed for good behavior. His sleeping bag resembled a cocoon, twisted and flattened by the weather, by camping trips with other thin-chested boys. Up close he examined the carpet checkered aqua and pink. His father snored. His mother sighed. It was almost a conversation: ruckus, exhaustion. When woken a panicked child he'd sat outside their bedroom door and listened and whispered back answers to imagined questions.

The oldest, sixteen, camouflaged by his parents' breathing, took the cardkey, found a gray-ponytailed man to buy paper-bagged bottles similar to those drunk in parked-car parks with his girlfriend back home. On the curb considering the slickness of the slickered girl in rollerblades, he felt lonely.

At the motel, the oldest woke his already-woken brother, led him to the mosquitoed pool, and sorry for themselves they wished for Meaningful Enough. A graduation, a career, a knock-out fuck.

Instead, their father with his last-chance vacation. The boys had voted for islands, for coasts, for nightclub nights and skipping to their twenties, for out of their parents' watch and care.

As the father collected roadside objects, the boys stepped back themselves. Ketchup-smeared napkins and coasters, splotched paper bags, stones and curbside sketches, flaps of fabric, wrappers. The mother, reluctant, handed up gutter nickels, bathroom-deserted lipsticks. The boys wondered what of their parents was contagious, what lay dormant inside them, what could spread again. Locked in a red van speeding toward history, the boys lay on bench seats, they closed their eyes, they listened.

Staring Contests

She sits on the brown carpet looking at me, two naked Barbies in front of her, but she isn't playing with them. I peek at her over my paperback, and she raises her eyebrows and lets out a gasp. Her cheeks turn pink, but she doesn't look away.

"Let's go to the school," I say. "You like the swings?"

She nods. She watches me stand, yawn, fix my ponytail, and then I stop with my hands in the air, my mouth open, and it's my turn to stare. This is a game I won't lose to a four-year-old named Lindy. Minutes go by. A bird caws outside. A car door closes, a woman talking, mad about yellowed grass. My arms ache. Lindy keeps her eyes on me, keeps me frozen as she gathers her Barbies. There's sand at the school, a big box of hard brown sand. The Barbies are going nude-beaching.

—✠—

Michael's at the apartment when I get home, the room smoky from hamburger grease.

"Five minutes too late!" he yells, meaning he's already started so I'll have to cook for myself.

"I told you not to bring that crap here anymore." I throw my book on the futon, then my purse, jacket, shirt, shoes, pants, bra, underwear.

"But you've got the good pan!" He kisses the air as I walk by.

"You're using the good pan? I bought that special for my veggies."

"I'm done. It's yours."

"You've got it all tainted."

In the bedroom, my robe's where I left it, slung over the seat of my chair. I pull it on, the knobby cotton soft and sweetly pungent with a couple weeks' sweat.

"I can't use it anymore," I say, back in the kitchen, watching the sleek black pan sizzle in the sink.

On the couch, Michael lifts his burger; ketchup plops to the plate. "It's just a job. You're taking it too seriously."

"What's wrong with taking it seriously?" I drop to the couch beside him.

He hums in pleasure as he chews, some made-up song. "Nobody serious has ever been happy. It's two ends of a continuum." He takes another bite and starts humming again.

—⁓—

Lindy on the playground is like Lindy at home: her world's a sphere with a four-foot diameter. She sits her Barbies on the ledge of the sandbox, their feet touching the sand but not breaking the surface. She leans back on her heels, watching them, leaning forward to adjust a bare, shiny limb this way or that, oblivious to the smack of the basketball, the girls dancing by the fence, the kid screaming obscenities on the swing: the reason we didn't go there in the first place.

The woman knitting beside me sighs. "His cat," she says, tearing long silver needles through the yarn so furiously it's hard to believe she's pulling something together. "I told him not to let it out. But his cousin *Roger* has an outdoor cat."

I nod in sympathy. Lindy has the dolls facing each other in the sandbox.

"I said if he's going to scream he's got to do it outside."

One Barbie reaches over and touches the hand of the other.

—∞—

"She's just in," Michael says into his cell phone the moment I open the door. He walks from the kitchen, jams the contraption into the crease of my shoulder. Kisses the air above my temple.

"Michael tells me you're watching your boss's kid every day."

I kick the door shut and glare at his back by the stove. I smell peppered meat. He's using the good pan. "Just an hour or two after work," I tell my mom. "Her husband's in the hospital. I'm getting paid for it."

"I thought you're getting paid to design brochures and recipe cards. God *bless* those furry animals! *Save them! Oh won't you save them?* And those little red peppers you draw just *so*."

I struggle out of my jacket, my shirt. The pants are tougher. I throw the phone down to unhook my bra and take off my underwear. "Ah," I sigh, picking up the phone. "What'd you say?"

"I said what about this kid? You're a professional baby-sitter now?"

"A little sympathy." I head toward the bedroom, where my robe lies in a crumpled pile on the floor. "God damn it!"

"Julia! Remember your anger scale."

"What do you need?" I ask, shaking out the robe, flapping it, snapping it against the chair, not looking for an event like last time, a spider on my leg.

"Dad's fixing the water heater again. This time every year, you remember."

"It's a good way to wake up."

"You know I don't need any help waking up. You should hear him, clinking and clunking around. It's giving me a headache."

"Did you want to come here?"

She clears her throat, "What're we having for dinner? Little red peppers?" She pauses. "You need to keep your phone on."

—៕—

"Just a short ride," I say, buckling her in, wondering if she's allowed up front, should she be in a car seat. But the sky's a murky gray and it's too late to worry. She looks small sitting there, a naked Barbie on each thigh. She adjusts the seatbelt so they're covered too, the rough nylon over their breasts.

"We're going to see Daddy," she tells them.

"That's right," I say. "It's bright in the hospital. You should've brought sunglasses."

"They don't have any sunglasses," Lindy says.

The nurse tells us where to go. The door's open a crack. The hall's bright but the room's dark inside, and we hear the soft rush of voices. Lindy tells her Barbies to be quiet as I push the door a few more inches and see my boss Sheila by the bed, her sharp red suit maroon and gruesome in the dark. She whispers to her husband.

"I've been cleaning out the basement. The boardgames in the icebox, half-filled with puzzle pieces. I found your marionette, the one from Switzerland."

"Freddy. He came with a whole bag of sausages."

"His legs are rotting."

"Sheila. They were rotting to begin with."

—៕—

My door opens before I turn the handle, and there's Dad, wearing a thick wooly beard and a red stocking-cap with white fur around the edges. "Trick or Treat!" he says, balancing a bowl of candy against his big velvet stomach.

"Damn." I look at him. "I think you're confused."

He picks out a Snickers and peels it open with one hand.

"We don't usually get kids in the building." I kick off my shoes and toss down my purse and jacket, but that's all I can do with my dad standing there. Michael and my mom are on the couch laughing, watching a sitcom.

"Good," he says, "I can't eat what you cook anyway."

"Why are you here?"

"Broke the water-heater." He fishes in the bowl. "They're fixing it later this week so we'll have to crash here a few days."

"Great. Wonderful." I head to the bedroom and close the door, lie on the bed in the dark.

"What was the girl for Halloween?" Michael asks in the doorway with a plate of spaghetti and big red meatballs.

"Sleepy, Sneezy, Painful, and Doc. And Hungry. All at once."

He picks my robe off the floor and drapes it over my reclining body. "Aren't you going to change?"

I sigh and turn toward him, curl up in a ball. He sits on the bed and offers me his fork. "It's Halloween," I say. "I guess I have to be someone other than me."

"Julia!" Dad yells and comes through the door with a grocery bag. "Look what I found in the closet." He turns the bag over and all my old shoes clunk to the floor.

"They're leather, Dad."

Mom follows him in and turns on the light, looks at the shoes.

"So what, they're leather," Dad says.

"I can't wear leather to work. I can't consume any animal products."

Mom asks, "What size are you?"

—⟋⟍⟍—

Outside on the street, leaves are falling, great spread-open hands on my face, my arms, and then gone to join their crumpled, crippled brothers on the ground. Across the street, a man walks his dog, a great white husky who doesn't notice me. I wait awhile. The man doesn't notice me either.

—〰—

I buy the Barbies some fuzzy blue hats.

"It's getting cold," I tell Lindy. She agrees and takes the hats. I help her put them on.

"What's wrong with your dad?" I ask.

She lays her Barbies on the carpet next to each other, their bare arms touching. She looks at me. She fixes her eyes into a stare. "His stomach is fat. It's full of animals."

Staring isn't a complicated matter: just a glazing of the eyes, a blurring of your focus so it's not in focus at all.

"He sneaked them. When Mom wasn't home."

"What kind of animals?" I ask, my eyes gently throbbing.

"Hams. Bolognies. Sausages."

—〰—

I hear the laughter come up the stairwell, walk down the hall; it stops in the hallway outside my door.

"You want to get that?" Michael asks, sitting on the couch between my parents. They're watching a documentary on flying, all in their pajamas.

I wash my hands and go for the door, smelling like baked eggplant but still in my suit, the only one of us appropriate for greeting.

"Surprise!" Two adult voices and one little squeak: my older sister and her husband and their three-year-old boy.

"Wow!" I say, smiling, but they're looking over my shoulder.

"We thought we'd find you here!" my sister says to my mom, who's walking toward them in white flannel pajamas.

"Grandma!" The boy jumps up and down. Everyone moves into the entryway.

"Why's your coat wet?" my dad asks my sister.

"It's snowing."

We go to the window and cram our faces into the frame, see the fine white shards flying, flickering beneath the lamps.

"You're just in time," I say. "The eggplant's almost ready."

—⟋⟍—

Sheila's waiting in my office; she's closed all the blinds; her skin's nearly blue.

"I want you to work on some new designs. Make winter squash seem interesting. Exotic. Is that possible?"

"Sure. I'm picturing a snowy land. Everyone outside, bright, shiny, and smoking pipes. Balancing huge chunks of squash on their forks."

She stares at the floor. "I'm sorry. It's been a lot lately. With Lindy."

"It's alright," I tell her. "You're paying me."

—⟋⟍—

We go to the school in gloves and scarves and hats. The days are shorter: it's 5:30 and nearly dark. The Barbies are freezing. I hear their teeth chattering, but they say the hats help. They help a lot.

Two girls are in the sandbox when we get there, playing a handclapping game, their bare red hands slapping sharply against each other, nearly sparking in the cold. But I suppose they're keeping warm enough from the contact.

The point is they're not even enjoying the sand. Lindy stands a couple feet in front of me, watching them, Barbies in hand. I watch them too, but the girls don't notice us. We stay that way for a while before I ask if she wants to go home.

—⟋⟍—

"What's wrong with him anyway?" Michael asks when we're alone in bed. My parents have gone; I'm back in my robe.

"Some stomach thing."

Michael sighs, his breath warm, smelling of meat.

"It could go on forever." I turn away from him and look out the window, the bare branches scarcely visible against the night. I get out of bed and wrench the window open, stand there a moment shivering, then strip the covers from the bed. Michael, purple and naked, watches me, pulls his knees to his chin.

I throw off my robe. I crash around the room, make it exotic.

—〰—

Lindy twists the Barbies together: heads on shoulders, arms around hips, thighs touching, shins and ankles twined around each other. Their eyes twinkle ecstatically.

She tells me, "They're in love. But something's happened." She won't tell me what; she shakes her head. "I'm sorry." She pulls on her coat, and I pull mine on, too.

The whole time we don't look at each other. We go to the school and take off the Barbies' hats, sit with our backs toward the kids and their basketball. With effort, we break the surface of the brown, frozen sand, dig deep with our thick-gloved fingers, much deeper it seems than the frame would allow. There's movement behind us, the ball punched into pavement and wood, the ringing of metal. We bury the Barbies in the sand. We leave the hats for someone else.

The Problem with Moving

One move leads to another move, and nowhere feels as good as you want it to feel; your childhood feels wrong, and this place feels wrong, and the next place feels wrong, and so you move again. Find a new job, a new apartment, meet a neighbor at the mailboxes; he has a dog named Kidney that terrifies you, but the neighbor is a new friend, the first one you meet and when he invites you to dinner you go because that's what you do, you've just moved to the area.

His wife is sullen with red wine, glancing at you, and you understand, you do not like people either, though she does not realize this about you because you chat with her husband like you do like people, and he chatters back nervously as though he really does like people; he is one of those rarities, only he usually pretends not to like them because of the wife. Hence the nervousness. He has broken a rule bringing you here. Kidney scratches behind a closed door down the hall.

Your job is in an office with bright yellow walls; they are too yellow, and you point to them and say you now know what it's like to work inside the sun. Everyone laughs, someone suggests we turn up the heat, and the next day someone brings you a bag of Sun Chips, then Sunny-D; soon they call you Sunny. You get a promotion. You go to the neighbor's to celebrate, and the wife,

takes Kidney for a walk. Neighbor tells you don't take it person-
ally. Neighbor is excited about the promotion.

Things slow down. Work. Coffee. Mailboxes. Neighbor. Your
coworkers sense something. They make calls, fix blind-dates for
your lunch hour, say: this might be the Moony you're looking for!
None of them are Moonies. You wish you could be friends with
the neighbor's wife who hates people, but you after all are a person, too.

Your mother calls. She says three houses opened up in their
neighborhood and they are all good deals. Your dad snores in
the background. Your mother says: I broke another plate today.
Your mother says: I ran into your high school sweetheart. No,
not married. Bald as a bat!

You move. Somewhere new. New neighbor, new job; it's not
hard, you are highly skilled. The walls are blue in the new office.
They call you Skyler.

New neighbor's dog Potato scratches down the hall. New
neighbor has no wife. You sleep together. You move in together.
Goodbye Potato. You tell your mother, she cries about it. At the
office they call neighbor Nightler. Things slow down. Nightler gets thin. You realize Nightler does not like people. He puts
headphones on when you enter the room.

Your coworkers sense something. You hear whispers around
his name. *Bzzzzzz Nightler bzzzzzz.* You close your door. Boy do
you miss old Neighbor.

Your mother calls, says: we're still here! Dad snoring. She
says: we bought new plates today. We bought three. One for you.

The problem with people: one person leads to another person, and no one's who you want them to be; even Mother feels
wrong, and Nightler feels wrong, and the next one feels wrong.

Nightler says: I'm hungry. I think you should leave.

You move. This time you move backwards. Hello Neighbor.
Hello Kidney. Hello wife that hates you. You say to Wife: I hate

you, too. You say to Neighbor: I do not hate you. I do not really hate everyone, only I think I do when I get restless. Will you chain me here to your kitchen chair? Will you be my Moony?

Wife leaves with Kidney. Goodbye. Goodbye. You are unhappy being chained down the rest of your life. But it's the only way to stop moving.

Blooms Lined Up Like This

Mid-March—that wet trampled month, time of rashes and sopping lawns and garden gloves changed constantly—the postcard arrived. Discovered by my thirteen-year-old son Mason back from an egg run to the corner store; he came into the kitchen heralding our mail piece by piece—Junk! Junk!—saving the postcard for last.

"Dear Frank, this is important," Mason read and then silently read the rest. The postcard pictured a lighthouse, so probably from my ex-mother-in-law's collection. But why addressed to my husband?

"If it's bad news, read it quickly," Frank said, retrieving Mason's backpack thrown by the door.

"Please stuff the postcard in the garbage disposal," I said. At our oak table thick as a butcher's block, I promised my day to a piece of paper. *Zodiac Flower Article. Review Season's Amaryllis.* I wrote monthly for *The Floriographer*, a comprehensive flower magazine I'd founded and then a year ago sold, though it had been much longer since I'd filled the house with fresh-cut flowers. I once fully supported the effort for true good moods; there remained vases in each room, in every cranny, empty. To write my articles these days I took my laptop to the community garden and on a bench pretended. New blooms! Fragrant sweet pea! Knock you out tulips!

Mason ignored me. The backs of his jeans were soaked to the shins and dotted with heel-kicked muck; he was pale and bleached and wore a necklace of red beads and shark teeth his father had left him in a pen-scratched will found beneath a pile of needles and torn-up matchbooks. Mason had a black bicycle he pedaled recklessly through the neighborhood; neighbors sometimes dropped by to wring hands over his gusto. I regularly grounded him to the sidewalks, though what could I do? For fun, his father had walked often in the gutter. Before Mason we were nearly impoverished, subsisting on heroin and plain pieces of white bread, our hearts dropped and wild, and Mason's father figured why not own the trope.

"I guess Grandma's dying again," Mason said.

"Please don't say it callously," Frank said. "You don't mean it like that." Frank was a child psychologist. He disciplined Mason with mock-sternness, a trying-out of fatherhood that didn't really fit. Though his lectures to Mason and me about what was possible in this life were consistent—Pleasantness! Happiness!—they were one reason—it drove me crazy—I loved him.

"What do you expect?" I asked Frank. "Every year's another death-sentence miracle." Harriet contacted me a couple times a year by way of handwritten letters and postcards, detailing her health and unmet expenses and memories she had of me beautiful, distant, and sad. *Come back to us*, she pleaded in one letter, and then boasted in the next: *I'm still alive. Don't need you in the slightest. Turns out I'm a miracle. You'll likely die before me. Ha Ha!*

"Flippancy about sickness is disturbing, emotionally," Frank said, nodding to my son.

Mason thumbed the postcard, watching me. "I wouldn't mind seeing a lighthouse for once in my sorry life."

"Your life's not an apology," I said.

"I wouldn't mind seeing one in my grateful life either."

Mason had become too much like his father lately—abrupt and distracted. I took the postcard from him. A lighthouse, a cliff, a sky darkening. Harriet's life obsession with such a helpful structure made as much sense as her pinched-cent affection for charities, her appreciation of the well-groomed viewed from her own falling-down house. When asked why lighthouses she sometimes moaned, "Because life's a dark stretch of shore!" When in a good mood she said, "Because I'm a lighthouse. A too-bright illuminator of everything."

On the back of the postcard, I didn't find the florid print I expected. The note was scribbled in green ink, my ex-sister-in-law's scrawl, the slant of icebergs. Kay wouldn't lie to us for her mother's sake. *It's reached the point,* the note said. *Three months.* And though it had lain dormant beneath the skin for years, on the postcard, among all the little words, *CANCER* stood out. Now the mailmen knew, too.

Harriet wanted us to spend a week with her in June for the death date. Would we please bring Mason and let a grandmother say Important Words to her grandson? *She's renting a house in the Outer Banks,* the card said. *She plans to visit some lighthouses.*

Composing my flower astrology articles required a certain exuberance this postcard didn't help. This month was the daffodil—generous, receptive flower of friendship and household happiness. I placed the postcard in the junk pile.

"Important words make me nervous," I said.

"The card's addressed to Frank," Mason said.

"Of course. They knew I'd throw it away."

Frank sorted out the broken egg shells and dropped them in the trash. Every weekend morning he insisted on breakfast. He believed in things like that—big meals, shared experiences.

"Some emotion is good for a childhood," Frank said. "It gives perspective."

"That's the problem between us," I said, meaning between me and everyone else. "You have positive associations. You look to the past and think Good, Useful, I'm glad. I look to the past and think something else."

"I understand you're not friendly with the past," Frank said. "But you don't want to ignore it entirely."

Like my ex, breathless, stumbling in the night into knocked-over flowerpots. Like my ex, dropped off at his mother's in the gray morning walking toward his sixth seventh hundredth recovery. Harriet was a part of my life when I needed a beacon of light, like a lighthouse is a remnant of what *used* to be useful. Now she was just this blocky structure disrupting my view of the shore.

—⁓—

Mid-April—month of mulch and lawnmowers and outside every house a woman with a spade—required a plan. Saturday morning and too much the same: Mason—store, Frank—breakfast, and me at the kitchen table listing important duties—*Clear Memory. Reboot. Rewrite. Dust Blinds.* A hopeless morning.

Frank was relentless about Harriet's Death Date. When he promised a breakfast surprise, I figured heart-shaped pancakes. I figured a lecture about sticking your wing outside your comfort zone, trusting no one will chop it off.

"It isn't healthy to fence yourself in," Frank said. "Seeing them won't ruin us. We're happy, aren't we?" He squeezed my shoulder. All these generic romantic gestures. I knew not everyone could be creative about it—it didn't mean Frank wasn't genuine, he just wasn't interesting.

In the door with Mason just back from the store: my ex-sister-in-law. Arriving unannounced in a denim jacket with leopard-like fur around the collar, Kay stomped chaos into the kitchen. She brought with her a mixed rose bouquet—early June's flower, flower of the Gemini—those clever adaptable flowers. Passion! Friendship! Virtue!

Kay dropped the roses in front of me, and mid-hug she sighed grandly into my neck. She lived in Durham, fifteen minutes from our house in Chapel Hill; often I saw her nest-hair at the counter in Elmo's Diner and backed out the door before she noticed me. Kay made me feel I was still one of them—hectic, phobic, important—all arms and closeness when she saw me, a big scene—We *miss* you! Her memories of my ex's chosen life shackled to his drug-addled cycles let me know she well-understood my decision to leave in the name of Mason—that tortuous path away from them, that curled-on-the-couch comfort of goodbye— though Kay often cried "If only you hadn't left!" while Frank stood beside me. "I'm here," I said, meaning North Carolina. Meaning reality.

Mason set the flour on the counter and a white dust floated and settled on the granite. Noticing anything too much reminded me of that life—gray rooms and white-laced flames, watching from my easy-chair throne my ex pass out and wake up panicked. Now every Saturday was Pancake Day. We always missed some essential component.

"I guess Grandma's really dying this time," Mason said.

"Go easy," Frank said. He gathered ingredients around the flour.

"I'll ride my bike to the beach," Mason said.

"I won't allow it," I said. "There's no sidewalk and no need to martyr yourself for someone you'll never see again."

"You've forgotten the purpose of a family," Kay told me, "which once called such is always such no matter the divorce or death in the equation." She pulled a bowl from the dishwasher and next to Frank cracked eggs messily. Only families made breakfast like this. I watched them.

"The three of you go," I said. "I don't want to see any lighthouses. I'll stay here and go to the garden."

"You know we like to pull together," Kay said. "There's a lot of good about us if you could remember it."

"Don't tell me anything good." Reluctance had purpose, evolutionarily. Creatures hid from larger creatures for a reason. It was always big emotions with them. My ex destroying himself in some way—collapsing in doorways, shaking beneath porch beams, picking his arms scabby—and then his drug problem's my fault, his ruined mind's my fault; everything's my fault for leaving him.

"I can't see her," I said. "She can't die in front of me." The Victorians sent messages in arrangements of flowers: a language, floriography, where certain blooms next to each other meant I Love You and others meant May You Suffer A Bloody Death. It was a relief knowing I wasn't the only one who confused the two.

"You're not the point of this," Frank said.

"You're right. I'm the blunt end of it." This month's astrological flower was the daisy—loyal, courageous Aries. It would have to be written about.

"We need you there," Kay said. "You fill a space that needs filled. No one else can fill it."

To the list: *Change Phone Number. Sell House. Move.* I was sure somewhere Harriet had a list, too, a list of all the lighthouses she wanted to see. I was sure I understood the pleasure of adding one more and one more, of filling up the whole space of a page and then starting another.

—⁂—

Mid-May, mid-decision. Month of sun-baked gardens and everywhere you look unstoppable growth. I should have gotten out my gloves and spade and headed outside like a true bloom lover, but I worried about how it would look, what it would mean if my garden didn't turn out too cheerful.

To Mason, Harriet was a saint. He sacrificed his body to the cause, inking himself with epitaphs in different-colored pens— *She Felt Often* and *She Was Tall For This Earth*—and spraining his wrist trying to jump over the iris-filled traffic island down the street. I remembered my ex, sleep-defeated, recovering from some binge in a couch corner mumbling accusations about his mom putting his dog to sleep, and chasing his dad toward death, and reminding them all of their own mortality to the point my ex always felt close to dropping off. Most nights Mason came home moderately bloodied. He perfected a far-off gaze when I spoke to him, when I snapped my fingers within millimeters of his cheek, when I shook his shoulders and said, "Do you hear me? Stay off the street! The street is a place for sad men!"

Frank brought home flowers—daisies, pansies, lilies white and scarlet—and positioned single stems in the tall glass vases crannied around the house. It was like when we first moved in, when I wrote about flowers and beginnings and it wasn't just a job, it was life. Frank wanted me to remember, but I'd lost it again; somehow, it was gone.

All month, Harriet called in the evenings wanting an answer, only I wouldn't allow the phone to be answered. Her messages accumulated, things like "There's a lot of good about dying . . . Come gather with us in black clothes and eat black food—olives, caviar, brownies . . . We're all victims waiting to be drowned . . . Piles of raisins . . . Goodbye Butterfly. Goodbye broken wing."

Butterfly. A name courtesy of Harriet for the times I left and flew back to them changed. Times of wrecked cuticles and car-packed belongings and baby Mason and me crammed into my Zeppelin-shrined room at my parents'. Then returned to a sleepless moth-eyed husband and a grandmother Mason called Bumpy—she used to bounce him on her knees and pretend they were on a great journey—until Mason turned three and he and I journeyed a different way. Away.

I made a lot of lists I didn't intend to make. A list started as *Top Summer Seeds* turned into *Necessary Beachwear*. A list started as *Possible Color Schemes* turned into *Probable Death Presents*. A list started as *Repel Pests Safely* turned into *Sterilize A Beach House*.

Soon it would be mid-June—month of family vacations looked forward to all winter, and the hassle of cars clogged with suitcases, cars laden with bikes and boogie-boards, and the misery of stand-still beach traffic suspended above The Sound where you could see the boats and jetskis of those already enjoying their vacation.

Of course Harriet wouldn't approve of Mason's behavior on the bicycle—"Don't bring into this house another life and death situation!" From the porch, she would watch over us: Frank and me unloading suitcases while Mason addressed his pent-up anger from five car hours of parenting by slamming his front wheel into the curb. He would perform an anger dance around it. "Take care of it, Butterfly!" Harriet would yell. Not thinner. Not paler. Not hairless. I imagined her how I most remembered her: propped up and pointing.

"You hope for the cathartic," I told Frank. We brushed our teeth together as a way to calm and connect after a day in the world. "But important words can do strange things to a person."

"I don't expect it to be easy," Frank said. "But you should believe more in the power of closure. Grieve strongly and it will be quick."

I spat. I felt like I owed someone an apology. The sorry past. The sorry future. Every month was another month I'd lived, and getting to the middle was hard and getting to the end was harder. Less than a year after the divorce, Harriet called me and said she found my ex dead in his room, crumpled by the window with the light coming in too bright on that side of the house. She said he called himself a ruined room this time trying to recover when he said he couldn't recover. She said his room's really ruined now. She wouldn't go into it.

"We should prepare for the worst," I told Frank. "Every time with this family I come back disordered."

Frank took my toothbrush and rinsed it and placed it in the plastic cup, which was molded at the bottom. "It will bring the three of us closer."

I held his hand. An off-and-on insomniac my whole life, I recognized the flashes, the irregular peaks of heat that meant I wouldn't sleep tonight. After this show the last three months— this pretending that when the date came around we might exist still in this house as we used to exist—I should've excused myself to the guest room. I should have lain perfectly still and admitted myself a ruined room.

Instead, I squeezed Frank's hand long enough he might feel a connection I might eventually want to feel, too. It was the month of the rose, but also of Cancer. Each month shared space with a hundred objects and names.

—ᴟ—

Mid-June. My ex's family crept in anyway: showed up for break-fast, sent themselves by mail, by phone, by way of my own troubled head. Unlike flowers, memories had a way of lining up you couldn't control. Unlike flowers, memories lived long after you cut them.

The night before the trip, I didn't sleep. I'd put off leaving, and now I wanted to go. I woke Frank and Mason, and we left when the streets were dark and quiet; the car was warm and on the highway driving fast felt like a dream. Nobody talked and nobody slept, though Mason had his pillow and lay beltless across the backseat.

An hour from the beach, the sun showed up and traffic increased. Frank told Mason to buckle his seatbelt, and Mason for once listened. With all the boats, boogie boards, and car windows painted *Here We Come Outer Banks* and *Jones Beach Trip Yeah!* it was apparent how morbid and wrecked our own vacation would be. Frank suggested we find a place to buy flowers.

"Let's keep going," I said.

"We should bring flowers," Mason said. To Frank and Mason, flowers were an empty gesture of kindness, of brightness. In Harriet's house a vase of red poppies had always stood in the middle of the dining room table. It was something I'd kept an eye on when we moved in for our recoveries; flowers were everywhere in that house: on window ledges, the sink in the bathroom, the television. I began to study the symbolism behind them and wonder: Why death flowers on the dining room table? Why resurrection lilies by the toilet? Why the daisy, flower of incorruptibility, by my pillow?

Frank found a grocery store. Next to the shopping carts in the crowded entryway, we found the black buckets, the suffocated bouquets in plastic sleeves. Limp. Prearranged. Meaningless. I selected ten and then in the parking lot with the early sun beating down, I discarded plastic and baby's breath crap onto the pavement. On the hood of our car, I got to work figuring out how to say everything I wanted to say.

Mason sat in an oil stain. "It doesn't have to be a masterpiece."

"The flowers are pretty much dead anyway," I said. "It's going to be a nice message."

"Just choose the best ones," Frank said. Everything was simple when you didn't know anything about it. I knew too much about everything.

An hour later, a bouquet lay beside Mason in the backseat. It was a mess. It said something like *I Love Hate Hate You. Leave Me I Miss You You're Going To Die Goodbye.*

"There's an hour of my life," Mason said. "Grandma will probably die before we get there." He rolled his window down so a screech accompanied us the rest of the way.

"It's a beautiful arrangement," Frank told me. But I didn't care what he thought.

The three-story beach house was bright pink clapboard and small round windows. Skeletal wood stairs and balconies hung from it like scaffolding. Harriet's real house had been ruin encouraged—her porch floorboards buckled and the pillars cracked and everywhere overgrown with bright green. Her narrow halls were fleur-de-lises molded. Her furniture was comfortable depressions.

This house looked just-built and shiny. Kay's car was already in the drive—they'd gotten in yesterday. Frank and Mason opened their doors and stretched, and I didn't move. "I'll stay here for now," I said.

Mason slammed his door and started for the house. Frank got the flowers out of the back and came around to my side.

"The entrance is the hardest part," he said. The ocean breeze blew into the car; it smelled like seaweed baked and rotting.

I moved slowly, laden with as many bags as I could carry. Mason had left the door open, and the two women stood in the entryway fawning over him. Harriet squealed when she saw me. She was rail thin and wore a blue and yellow parrot scarf around her head.

"I'm dead already, Butterfly! You missed it. I died this morning."

Kay came over and helped me with the bags. "Hi insect who flies." She kissed my cheek, and her face next to mine was an oven. She hugged Frank. "Thanks for bringing her."

"I'm allowed to die as many times as I want," Harriet said. "You'll get used to it. I fall over a lot. I sleep all the time. When the real death comes you'll say, 'Ha Ha Harriet's joking again,' and it will feel like a joke. Which is how it should feel."

I hugged her. I didn't want her to die. She held onto my hand.

"Finally we've got her." Kay put her arm around me. "You're in time for breakfast. We'll make it together and then walk on the beach."

"And then quickly to the lighthouse," Harriet said. "Everything must be done fast and exactly how I want it."

The two of them led me deeper into the house. "It's a big place," Kay told me. "You could destroy one room and then move into another."

They were so bright and forceful. There were flowers in the house, but we didn't need them. The rooms were tall and wide, and on the beach side of the house there were no walls, only windows, and outside the windows the waves rushed onto the shore. There was only the small regret knowing I was a part of them and had been away so long. Somewhere behind us were the others.